COL

Ann Mynard (née Lawrance) grew up on the Foxash Land Settlement in the early years after the war. As a young child she spent much time with the other smallholding tenants, and passionate about animals, helped tend their livestock.

Later, married to Keith and with children, Angela and Philip, in 1965 the family moved to West Sussex, where Ann assisted her husband in running his typesetting business.

Always keen on horses, Ann rode for other people until she finally acquired a horse of her own and spent many happy years riding over the Downs.

Ann, now widowed, lives close to her family and finds life busy helping her four grandchildren, and writing.

Then there is always Mason the black Labrador to take her for a walk.

LAND
SETTLEMENT

Ann Mynard

Land
Settlement

Vanguard Press

VANGUARD PAPERBACK

© Copyright 2005
Ann Mynard

A CIP catalogue record for this title is
available from the British Library

ISBN 1 84386 160 7

Vanguard Press is an imprint of
Pegasus Elliot MacKenzie Publishers Ltd.
www.pegasuspublishers.com

First Published in 2005

Vanguard Press
Sheraton House Castle Park
Cambridge England

Printed & Bound in Great Britain

Dedication

To those who live and work at the still
thriving Foxash Land Settlement.

Acknowledgements

To John Ashdown for all his support

And thanks to (Mrs) Claudia Gould, writing tutor, for her encouragement

Chapter 1

1952

ON THE Essex/Suffolk border where he now lived, Jim Macaulay, at thirty-eight, found himself often referred to as 'Old Macaulay'. This had disconcerted him at first but as time went on he recognised the term to be one of some affection rather than of derision. In this part of the country, the word 'old' could be used admiringly, but if 'bloody' was put in front of it, he had discovered it meant quite the opposite. Nonetheless, Macaulay found much comfort in the way he now seemed to be accepted as the landlord of the 'Wooden Fender'.

It hadn't always been so easy. In the shadowy days after Pat's sudden death, he had struggled to continue with his job as barman at the Wagon and Horses. It took him out of the now silent home he had once shared with her and gave him company and conversation, but the lonely stillness when he returned and opened the door had devastated him. Slowly losing a hold on his job, he'd slipped from despair into depression and when his boss had finally to "have a talk with the man or we soon won't have a customer left," Jim Macaulay knew he would have to get away to start a new life if he were ever once more to find some measure of peace or contentment.

Among the few properties for sale with the estate agents in Colchester, where Jim had placed his old home, was a small cottage of a public house just nine miles away. Catching sight of the details in the window as he left the estate agents, he turned on his heel and went back inside to find out more. The inn was isolated, out on the open road from Ardleigh and further along still from its nearest neighbour, the bakery at the outside edge of the village. The previous owner had retired. The isolation, and the possible lack of customers in such an out of the way public house might have contributed to his early retirement, Jim thought; still, no harm in just taking a look.

The inn stood solidly before him as it had stood all the long years since it had been built. As he looked up and surveyed the building, he noted the sagging middle of the roof wandering underneath a single tall chimney, the stack leaning slightly more than looked safe. The loose-leaf windows upstairs and down were set solidly four-square on each side of the sturdy wooden door, though all the oak wood was dry ridged, and naked of paint. There were even, glory be, yellow roses arching defiantly out from the old wall in a windswept tangle, regardless of the only too apparent neglect. Surely, after all this time, it wouldn't fall about his ears the moment he moved in. Feeling more enthusiastic than he had for a long time, he began to think seriously about taking the pub on. Perhaps he might strike a bargain he could afford.

Now, four years later, he had built some kind of a new life where he felt he belonged. People had become used to seeing him walk by, hat low over his eyes while he peered under the brim, his pipe well-primed and going strongly, a little black lurcher ghosting along at his heels. He knew the locals had found him shy at first, barely nodding when he passed his neighbours in their gardens after their long day at work. The tenants must have thought him something of a loner, but as time went on they became friendly with the quiet, diffident man, and even if he didn't smile as much as a landlord should, there was always a genuine welcome for them in his tiny pub. He kept a huge fire in the hearth in winter, though he had quickly removed the token 'wooden fender' which was there when he'd first seen the small main saloon. "Didn't want to burn the bloody pub down with a spark from one of them there fires he has," said Ed Spendley, one of the two odd-job men, stopping off in the pub one lunchtime from scything the roadside verges.

However, Jim felt concerned that, in removing the wooden fender, he might have removed a long tradition as well. "Did I upset anyone? You know, throwing that fender out." He passed a pint along the bar to Reg Clarke, the senior of the two workmen, who grasped the dimpled glass in a rough brown hand and conveyed it swiftly to his parched lips. An answer from him would have to wait.

"Gawd no, had to happen," said Ed, surfacing from his nearly drained glass with a sigh. "Anyhow, the old wooden fender, the one this place's named after, is that fence across the road. Joe uses it to keep his cattle from falling in the pond when they come to drink, or for calling in here for a beer. Isn't that so Reg?" Reg raised his glass and took another sip, then lowered it to study the froth moving steadily back from the brim. "Barred, they be!" said Reg, contentedly.

Chapter 2

Peter Starling sat at one of the rocky wooden tables nursing a Guinness in his huge brown hands. Lost in his thoughts, his broad head low, he stared sullenly at the carpet beyond the table.

"Don't see you in here this time of day, Peter," Jim called across to him. The truth was Jim had never seen the baker in his pub before and, since he lived just up the road, Jim thought he must be teetotal or something. He knew he was always busy, together with that poor, pretty wife of his, baking bread and buns and icing cakes. He supplied all the tenants with everything a baker could bake. Why he didn't try to get some help in there Jim couldn't think. He must be making quite a living since he was the only baker in the long Land Settlement area between Ardleigh and Lawford.

Peter glared back, picked up his half-drunk pint and swallowed the rest, then, wiping his fist across his mouth, he got to his feet. "Do I have to clock in and out now then?" and he walked out leaving Jim open-mouthed and wondering quite how he'd offended the baker with such an innocent remark.

Ed Spendley, back for his evening pint along with Reg, slowly lowered it onto the adjoining table. "How that little wife of his sticks it in that lonely old place with him and no social life to speak of, I don't know. She always looks worn out."

"Well, you should hear my Mary go on," said Reg with a laugh. "There's no talking to her at the end of a big washday, she's that tired. We sit either side of the fire and doze off. We have to wake ourselves up to go to bed, but at least we can laugh about it."

They all went quiet for a while. It was often said that hard work never killed anybody, but some of the older men were bent from long days in the fields, with the corners of sacks split open and spread across their backs to take the brunt of cold, wet rain while they sliced the green tops from the sugar beets, grasping the muddy, cold root vegetables with stiff hands, the blade falling inches from their fingers. There were a few fingers missing too when hands got so cold they couldn't be felt and the knife went too close. The men considered that job one of the worst of the year's work cycle.

Sugar beet was one of the usual crops grown since the war when sugar could not be shipped from abroad, and in 1952 it was still a predominant crop in the flat East Anglian fields.

Philbert Wright roused his old bones from his corner chair by the fire where he had been slowly sifting through Peter's truculent reply before he'd stormed off. These days, Philbert was regarded as one of the necessary pub fixtures since it had apparently become his second home. He sat a bit straighter to give a rare opinion. "What do he want to get hisself so worked up for then? It were a fair question, Jim. Bloody old fool!"

Chapter 3

Peter Starling lurched out of the Wooden Fender regretting his bad temper, but he had felt hounded enough before he went in there for a pint. It seemed however hard he worked and however long the hours he put in, Sally wasn't satisfied. There was a coolness between them of late that he couldn't seem to get beyond. She went about helping him at the bakery as she always had and, considerate husband as he was, he was careful to see she didn't lift too heavy trays and he gave her plenty of time off to get the house straight and see to the dinner and such. Couldn't she see that he was working so hard to ensure a good future for them both? There had always been Starlings at this bakery since anyone could remember. He had taken over from his father, having learned the trade when he left the village school, and his parents had saved enough for a good retirement. The only time he was away from the bakery was during the war years when he was called up. Then he was pressed into the catering section to bake for his Army comrades for the entire duration of the War. Now he was glad to use his strength and know-how to work hard in his turn to carry Sally and himself along.

He thought back to the days when he and Sally were in the same class at school. He was always big for his age and he knew she admired his good looks and strong body. While he basked in her attention, he knew she had a soft spot for him with her shy glances when they met; the talking with smiles that dissolved into self-conscious laughter. Later, when he saw her walking her father's dogs, he had asked her to go to see a film with him in the town. She had stood gazing up at him, eyes wide in a serious face, already lost in girlish expectations. Her reply that she "might be free then," in an attempt not to appear too keen, fooled no one.

From then on, all his free time after helping his parents was spent with Sally. Walking, cycling, swimming in the river, wherever he was, so was she. At eighteen he went off to Aldershot to do his National Service, and Sally and he exchanged longing letters while they waited for him to come home on leave. He remembered how thrilled they both were when they met each other again after the weeks apart. Those teenage years when they grew together, he led and she followed. He called the tune and she danced to it, besotted by him while he thought her the prettiest little thing he'd ever seen. One day he called such a merry tune he danced her right upstairs while her parents were out and when they returned too soon or, as her parents thought, too late, their wedding day was quickly arranged. Peter was sure he'd wed the only girl in the world for him.

All that was twelve years ago. 'What was happening now?' he wondered. He reached home at 8 o'clock to find Sally knitting in the brown chair by the fire. She barely looked up when he walked through the door but the clicking of the needles seemed sharper and faster as she said, "There's some soup for you in the saucepan on the stove if you're hungry."

He stood still, his arms hanging, and stared at the top of her fair hair bent over the knitting. "Soup? Soup! That's no meal for a man who's been doing the heavy work I have all day! And you sit there knitting! If you've time for that you've time to do me a bit of supper."

She looked up at him at last. "I put bacon and egg on the table while you were out at the pub, but I have been hard at it working today too, you know, and if it isn't good enough, then go and eat some of that precious bread you're always baking."

"What the hell's got into you woman?" he exploded. "You know everything I do here is for both of us. It's our livelihood; you know that. We both work hard. Why are you like this?"

19

"Like what?" Sally threw the knitting down and sprang to her feet. "There's always this awful pressure, day in day out, get the bread out, no time to live or just be! I'm always tired and so are you. Don't you realise? Our life is now, not in years to come."

"You're mad, you never used to nag. I take the brunt of the work and give you time to do your housework and such," he said, waving his hand round the room. "Do you think anyone has leisure to do just as they please, my girl? Of course not! The job has to be done, I thought you always understood that."

"Well, of course I know that, but couldn't we just get away for a while?"

Peter stood amazed. Where on earth did she want to go?

"We used to have days where we simply cycled and picnicked," Sally said wistfully. "We went to the pictures, or just walked. Now, it's you working all day and delivering the orders late at night – it's a wonder they all wait up for you, you're so late sometimes."

Peter, quieter now, turned on his heel and went to the kitchen. There was no talking to her when she was like this. He'd have to get something for himself now and perhaps she'd come to her senses in the morning. There was courting then there was marriage. They didn't have to go out anywhere now they had a home of their own, and besides, like she said, they were too tired to go cycling and such these days. Maybe they could take the van to the coast on Sunday when they shut for the day. Perhaps she'd be happier after that.

Sally sat thinking hard after he'd left the room. Was she being unreasonable? She knew when they married that the bakery would be their life as well as their livelihood. Other women seemed to manage the flat, unvarying days, but a lot of them had children to take the routine and monotony away. There was more of a purpose with young ones about who depended on you, and more coming and going, but after all these years of marriage, there had been no hint of a baby for them, nor had Peter mentioned his disappointment. If she ever enthused over a new baby in the neighbourhood, he'd be quiet and reticent. She had thought he was like a lot of men in her family, who appeared to take a manly stance against discussion of what they considered to be a woman's subject. She had simply decided there was plenty of time later when they'd got more modern equipment in the bakery and less to do maybe, just a bit more time on their hands to look around.

The trouble for her had always been that where Peter was concerned, she had constantly followed his lead. She had always thought the world of him and he knew it. They were both very young when they hurtled into marriage, which back then they seemed light heartedly to take on as an irresistible adventure. Now she wondered if he had really felt as strongly for her as she did for him. He had been taking her for granted for quite a while now, and it was time she had a say in things too. She did not quite see how she could achieve much independence after twelve years of so much going Peter's way, but she was growing up enough to see things more clearly.

She mused on long after Peter had gone huffily upstairs to bed. He would expect everything back to normal by the morning, she knew.

On the following Sunday, when Peter backed the van out to the front of the bakery, he discovered a knocking noise in the engine and when Sally came out to see what was going on, he was desperately diving under the bonnet of the old van, muttering fiercely. He looked up, red-faced, as she stood there and said he must get the van right for work the next day now while he had the time to do it. He was sorry but the trip to the coast was off – they couldn't risk getting stranded there, could they? Sally had been looking forward to getting away from the place for a day, just the two of them to talk things over and maybe agree to have a bit of help now and then. Now she could see a morning of holding spanners and making tea and giving the commiseration that she found most wives offered on these occasions. Irritated and disappointed in equal measure, she decided that it was Peter's fault he was now driven to cope with the wretched van. Why hadn't he used some of the money they were earning to buy a more up-to-date one? Just where did all the money go that they had been working together for all this time? In the early days of their marriage when she had with lighter heart asked just such questions, there had always been the sensible reply that they should save all they could in case they needed some unexpected cash to tide them over. She had carelessly agreed, trusting him and his judgement. He had held the purse strings until it was a habit.

"Look, Peter, there's really no point in my staying around here when I can't really help, I think I'll just walk along to Mum's for a chat. I'll take a bag and see if I can find a few blackberries along the way. They'll make a change. I'll cook us something this evening when I get back."

Peter looked up from the bonnet of the van and stared. "What am I going to do for midday, then?" he asked.

"There's some more of the bacon and you can fry an egg or two with that," she replied, and turned on her heel to set off along the road. She had put on one of her 'good' dresses thinking they were off to the seaside and the black shoes she had just polished, but when she saw some large blackberries lying thickly along the other side of the narrow ditch beside the road, she risked reaching across to pick a few. Just as she stretched too far and missed her footing across the ditch, Jim Macaulay closed the lychgate of the Ardleigh churchyard and saw her pinned by her dress to the brambles, and struggling to get herself out of the ditch. He moved fast along the road to assist her, then smiled as he watched her recover herself and re-pin her hair which had caught in the brambles and tumbled down. She had taken great trouble to dress her hair up this morning and struggled to put it right again.

It was a long time since he had just stood and admired a woman as he did now. She stood at the roadside looking rather cross, he thought, her bodice tight against her breasts as she fought to lift her heavy fair hair back into a topknot and pin it.

22

She shook the skirt of her cream coloured dress to straighten it and looked up at him. She caught his admiring glance before he reddened and shyly looked beyond her and away and she was touched. How odd that although he'd been their neighbour for so long, she had only caught glimpses of him up to now across the field that separated their homes. He stood tall and slim, the red now faded from his lean jawline and . . . 'sailor with the navy-blue eyes', now where did that spring from? Yes, she'd heard he'd once been a submariner. Those eyes looked back at her discerningly and it was Sally's turn to blush. Straightening herself, she was about to wish him a belated 'Good morning' then continue on her way, when he asked "Where are you going to, my pretty maid?" his head slightly inclined, smiling gently with the question.

"I'm off to see my mother, if I ever get there – sir," she said, smiling back.

He gave a small bow, turning away, as he said, "And I have to get back to open the pub for the midday crowd. Sunday is usually quite busy before they go home to their dinners." She turned to go and he called, "Strange we hardly ever meet, even though we are next-door neighbours, just down the road from one another."

She waved as she set off again and wondered how he managed on his own with a pub to run and then cooking and cleaning for himself. It certainly wouldn't do for Peter.

Chapter 4

Bob and Jean Carden, Sally's parents, and Bella and Tom across the road from them had been close friends as well as neighbours ever since they'd moved into these Land Settlement houses.

The Land Settlement was an association first set up in the years between the Great Wars. Some said it was a government brainwave to create new rural employment after the farming slump of the 1930s. Here, each semi-detached house was surrounded by a parcel of land for a tenant to farm pigs, chickens, goats, vegetables and fruit. In addition, between each holding was a small field, producing grain or potatoes to be harvested by the Association's overall employees using horses or tractors. All of this produce was collected at the central packing shed, graded and sent on lorries to Covent Garden under the LSA label. This, in essence, was what the system was all about.

For some of the men desperate enough in those hard times to take on whatever job they could find wherever they could, it was a baptism of fire. Here, families from all over Britain – from Wales, the Midlands, Ireland, and the North – suddenly found themselves thrown together with a common aim, and uncommon accents and ways of expressing themselves, into a freshly mixed melting pot. They launched themselves into a rural way of life, farming in a small way, becoming the backbone of a new community. For some, it was their first taste of rural life and farming. No one made a fortune – far from it – but the camraderie engendered formed many lifelong friendships in the doubtful comfort of their all being in the same boat.

To the astonishment of most people in this particular

community on the poor Essex soil just bordering Suffolk, the enterprise actually worked!

Bob, who had studied at agricultural college, took up the post of Overseer which entailed looking after the health and pruning of the vast orchards of apples, pears, plums and later the lifting of potatoes on the surrounding enterprises also attached to the central packing shed.

The whole season started with gooseberry picking, on to strawberries and blackcurrants, then the tree fruits. He used a Land rover to visit all the orchards and livened up his life with two black Labradors, Bess and Mac, who seemed to live for outings in the back of the Land Rover. They stoically accepted being thrown about as Bob drove over the rough ground between the trees while looking for any diseases or pests. If he took his shotgun with him, the two dogs were delirious with joy and Bob was obliged to keep them strongly in check. They must sit still and quietly when the gun went off, then bring back any game he shot to put gently down at Bob's feet. The competition between the two was keen but good-natured, the essence of a happy breed. When Bess had puppies from time to time, Bob always found homes for them quickly, even though few tenants had very much money to spare to feed a dog.

It was the women who picked the fruit when each variety became ripe throughout the year, though it was heavy work. The supervisors and managers jobs were invariably given to the men; those who were often disabled or too old to go to war. They kept the grass and weeds down, tied up the raspberries and blackberries and dug and tended the greenhouses. Some of the women worked in the greenhouses pricking out tomato seedlings, a principal crop. Huge stacks of them were loaded on tractors to be taken to a central packing shed where they were put onto noisy running rollers and graded by a line of women.

Pigs were kept centrally, near the packing shed, along with the billy goat which was lent to the tenants. Some of the young children on the estate would gather acorns from the wood nearby to feed the pigs where they were housed in wide pens and allowed to go in and out of their sheds as they chose. The billy goat needed a bit more restriction and contented himself by suddenly jumping up above his closeboarded pen. He would frighten the lives out of the unsuspecting youngsters busy feeding the piglets when he hung his long, bearded white face over the fence and snorted. The children soon learned to keep away from him when he was tethered out. He would threaten to butt any who came near enough and his smell was fearsomely strong.

Many of the tenants liked to rear their own pigs on their smallholdings, and there was a large Saddleback boar and later a Large White boar kept for anyone to use for their own pig-breeding. Most tenants kept chickens as a matter of course and there was always swapping of vegetables, eggs, flowers – anything surplus, between the neighbouring tenants to benefit everyone.

Chapter 5

Bella and Jean, now in their late fifties had, like all the women around the Land Settlement, worked physically hard all their lives.

Bella was pleased she didn't have to share a garden pump with her next door neighbour as her mother had – she had taps at her kitchen sink indoors, and an airing cupboard. She did still have the outside lavatory to contend with, just as her mother had and quite envied Jean on the other side of the road. She had a flush toilet indoors! One of the perks of an Overseer's life, she supposed. Jean even had a bathroom, but the houses on Bella's side still had a bath under a wooden lid at the far side of the kitchen. Even so, for Bella, this was a welcome step up from when her mother used to take the tin bath from the pantry wall and fill it with water from the range for the once-a-week baths. How on earth had Mum managed?

Jean popped across the road to see her one afternoon for a cuppa and a chat. Bella thought she seemed a little unhappy. She put the kettle on the cooker hob and went to the little walk-in cupboard for some cherry buns she'd cooked the day before.

"How lovely to see you Jean, I've been wanting a chat all week, but we do seem to be always on the go, don't we?" said Bella, bustling.

Jean settled herself by the black range and looked up as Bella came in with a tray of tea things. "Bob's been out a lot lately seeing to the apple and pear picking, even on Sundays sometimes, just to check that baskets and ladders and such are shifted to the next orchard in time for the pickers," said Jean. "It's given me a bit of time to get some sewing finished, I suppose – and then Sally turned up last Sunday out of the

27

blue." Bella passed her a cup and a plate with one of the buns and waited.

"She didn't seem too happy, rather upset, because they were planning to go to West Mersea and then that van of his wouldn't go, and I think she was somewhat fed up." Then Jean sat up a bit and burst out with, "Fancy her leaving Peter and walking off like that, not like her at all!" The cup rattled in its saucer as she held it, and she set it down beside her as she went on more calmly, "Sally did seem a bit tired and pale, though she'd walked a fair way, I suppose. A trip to the sea would have done her good."

Bella had known Sally all her life, had watched her grow up. It seemed that suddenly there was Peter on the scene, then a wedding when she was very young. She had quietly wondered if there was a baby on the way, but there had been no family then, or since. She had overheard the odd comment from time to time about what a taskmaster that Peter Starling was. She was glad Elsie had married a considerate man like Alan. They both seemed to be happy and she found him easy-going herself.

"Perhaps you could invite them to a meal with you and Bob soon," suggested Bella. "Sally might be glad of the break and it would get them both out, and away from baking for a change!"

Jean smiled, "That's a good idea," she said, and thought it would give her a chance to see if there was anything worrying them. Looking more cheerful now, Jean relaxed and asked, "Have you heard any more about next year's 'do' up at the hut?"

"Mrs Morgan next door says there's to be quite a celebration for the Coronation next year," said Bella. There had been a lot of news on the wireless about the new Queen since poor King George VI had died in February. Women's weekly magazines had carried what Bella considered to be articles too well-sugared about the Royals in practically every issue lately but it kept them up-to-date from a certain viewpoint. The papers had given more factual news and it

28

seemed that most areas of England were going to make a bit of a splash. Bella remembered the old hut shaking, with everyone in the district who could gather there on VE night letting themselves go at last in celebration. She still had the large navy straw hat with big white bows and a half-veil decorated with little navy 'v's upstairs, safely wrapped. It had been an unheard of extravagance, but it had suited the occasion. She hoped the whole estate would join in to make the Coronation celebrations something that everyone could look forward to and enjoy.

Jean, her mind still on more immediate concerns, brought Bella back to the present with, "Bob says there's something wrong with the rabbits he sees out now and again. He's heard they have some disease or other and they're so dopey, he's able to bump them off quite easily. It's nasty and I don't fancy any rabbit pie. He says its myxomatosis, and it was spread deliberately!"

"Tom said something like that not so long ago, Jean," replied Bella. "We'll all miss a good rabbit stew, and Tom more than most. Let's hope it'll soon be over."

Both women fell to discussing the measurements of some blue curtaining Jean was sewing for Bella, but Bella was wishing her friend had some grandchildren to enliven her life for her. Bella found hers to be a constant source of delight and interest. Well, of course, it was an absolute godsend that they all lived near enough to call on her often and she could watch them grow up.

Jean walked back to her home a little more cheerful for the talk with her friend, planning to ask Peter if he and Sally would like to come and have dinner at the weekend. She'd ask when he called with the loaves later that day.

Bella went out to mix some chicken meal and to call her Rhode Islands in off the stubble where they were stretching their legs and gleaning a few grains still left from the harvest. When they stopped laying, around Christmas time, she would have the awful job of deciding which one to kill for the Christmas dinner. It was a job she and Tom had done between them for years now. He killed the chicken and plucked it, she drew it and prepared it for cooking. She would sometimes let one good layer go on for the next year to mother day old chicks or sit on fertile eggs which she bought from the WI shop in Colchester. She had kept one or two fine cockerels. Boogie, her favourite, had shimmered with green and red feather cascades, but he had seemed a bit slow when a rat was about near the henhouse. Now she used a bantam cock – all scrawn and courage – and the hens were delighted with him.

She shut them all in their shed and went indoors to get a meal together for Tom who was due home soon.

Chapter 6

Bella smiled, happy at the sight of two young heads bent together over their paintings on the kitchen table. William seemed to have grown up a lot in the past year and at nine years old had stolen a great march on his younger brother Barry who, at five years was going through one of his awkward phases again. She put a mug of cocoa down beside each paint tin. They had to have a paint tin each, it was bedlam if they had to share.

"Look, Gran," they both spoke at once, and William's picture, so neat and detailed of aeroplanes and helicopters crowding a blue sky with a smiling sun was indicative of his leaning toward things engineered. Barry's strong walking bear reminded Bella of his love of animals. She would ask for both pictures to put them in the kitchen on the wall with the others already there.

The cocoa always went down quickly, and both boys brought her the mugs and grinned behind black moustaches. "Look at my muscles, Gran," said Barry and putting his thumb in his mouth and blowing, pumped his arm up and down while seeming to inflate his skinny little arm. "Well, I wish you were strong enough to turn the mangle handle for me," Bella shot back. "I'm afraid you'll both have to clear the table now, boys, I must set it for dinner, your Grandad and Mum will be in soon and I daresay you're both hungry."

Monday mornings, washing day, were always a drudge, she thought. The performance of lighting the boiler in the shed (first find some thin dry sticks and paper) and filling with buckets from the kitchen tap, each one carried across the path from the kitchen door. It took a long time for the boiler to heat sufficiently for the sheets to go in, then to cool enough for the other clothes. Well, today was a fine September one, starting dewy and cool, the sun beginning to rise. She loved these mornings when the sheets soon blew dry on the line from the wind gusting across the field beside the house.

She cut some cold pork from Sunday's roast and mashed the potatoes. There was still some green tomato chutney left from last year's batch to go with the beetroot she'd been slicing. There was a large spotted dick pudding quietly huffing on the stove to go with some custard – an easy dinner after a busy morning washing.

She wondered how her daughter was getting on at her interview for a solicitor's secretary in the village and was in two minds about this. Not many wives had jobs outside the home but Elsie seemed to need more than the usual round of washing, ironing, cooking and clearing up for everyone. She wondered how any young mother could find the spare time to do it.

Elsie propped her bicycle against the kitchen wall and came grinning into the room. The boys erupted with exaggerated excitement at seeing their mother arrive. "I did get the job, Mum", she said breathlessly. "I start on Monday when these two go back to school". Bella smiled, hiding her doubts, and wished her daughter good luck. Susan three houses down, would bring them home with her from school and at fourteen years old and soon to get a job herself, seemed a steady enough girl to look after them till Elsie arrived home and Susan could earn a little pocket money in the meantime. She would always help out herself, of course.

Elsie called to William as he orbited the room with his picture now folded into a paper aeroplane, humming to himself while he held it high before zooming it down with a growl in his own Battle of Britain, "Come and give me a hand setting the table, there's a love." William sighed and helped his mother take the cutlery from the open table drawer to set round. Bella called to Barry, "Wash your hands now," and later "No, both of them – yes I know only one had paint on." She sighed, "How on earth you can contrive to wash one

32

hand without the other I don't know. It must be so hard trying!"

There was a lively charge to the table just as Tom came in. He'd been ploughing between the houses in the row. He wasn't usually so handy to home as today. Bella had waved to him as he went back and forth past the side window and the boys had 'crazed' her (she said) to be out on the tractor with him, but if the boss should chance past in his Land rover and see this frivolous behaviour, Tom would have been in trouble. He would have had to 'use eyes in the back of his head', to watch the two boys. It would have been so easy for their small hands to stray near the great wheels turning under the narrow grey mudguards. Accidents on the smallholdings did happen from time to time however closely the children were watched.

Tom took his place at the head of the table and frowned at the two boys who grinned back disarmingly. "Have you two been good this morning, then?"

They knew he would ask that – he always did. It would be the day when they said "No", William thought. But he would never dare. Gran and Grandad didn't allow for much cheek! "Mum's starting a new job," said Barry, "so we'll be left to do as we like!"

"I doubt it," replied Tom, comfortably. "I bet she's got it all sorted and you two with it, more likely." He forked some potato into his mouth and settled down to his meal. That old grey tractor had a pretty hard seat and he was glad to have a break, though he was grateful for a dry, sunny day. He could turn over the stubble much quicker when the earth was dry.

He knew some of the tenants missed seeing George Springett walking up and down with the two Suffolk Punches the Settlement had always used. George had been ploughing with horses on the estate for forty years and on his retirement last year there was a unanimous vote by the management to keep the horses in retirement so long as George could still look after them. Tom had been amazed. He could not remember a time when such a move had been made but

33

George and his wife were a very popular couple, devoted to each other, and George looked after his horses as he would have his children, had they had any. He was just as tolerant of the one or two youngsters who ran after him when he harvested with the big sails flailing the corn, the stooks ejecting out of the back end of the machine, while he sat on the side talking softly to the two pulling horses. Then, in autumn, the children had to walk fast to keep up with the old man when he took the plough up and down behind the big striding horses and they soon gave up.

"What does Alan think of all this work you're taking on then, Elsie?" Tom asked, looking up from his dinner.

"He knows how set I am on getting out and earning us a bit more, Dad" she replied quietly, "And we agreed in the end that I give it a try. It's not far to cycle and Mr Timothy seems to be a friendly man. He said not to worry about anything, but to ask him if don't know, as everything legal must be accurate. I think I will like the challenge." Tom thought about this. He was quite sure he would be somewhat put out if Bella took it into her head to go out to work. They had always managed to get by on what he earned and he thought Elsie had enough to do with running her home with the two little boys. "Oh, I have to be very discreet, too, Dad as it looks like I shall be seeing a few neighbours and friends we know, it's usually trouble when people need a solicitor," added Elsie.

"Hmm, I expect you'll see how it goes," replied Tom non-committally.

"Barry," said Elsie suddenly with some asperity, "if you don't want your food, don't wave your fork in the air, just leave it on the plate!"

"Can I get down? asked William, shuffling on the edge of his chair. "May I get down sounds better," said Elsie, now into her stride, and don't go too far, we have to walk back home soon."

There was a wild bolt for the door, they would get as far as they could in the time they had. The piggery, now it was empty of pigs and quite clean was a favourite just at the top of the garden. There were lots of stored hay bales, too. They made great hiding places when they were moved about – in fact the boys could use them for many games as long as they didn't break the bales. Then Grandad was inclined to growl that they would not be allowed in there again. Mr Bowles the boss would soon put a stop to it if he found out. Both boys, by unspoken consent, began moving the bales to build a den as they had many times before, sometimes bringing apples and drink to invent games in a world of their own, without adult interference.

Bella and Tom's other two grandchildren, Alex, now five years old and Rosie who was only two, lived near enough to often visit. Alex liked to climb the hollow oak tree near the piggery, refusing to heed Rosie's shrieks of indignant frustration as she stood underneath, until she was led away to help Bella with the chickens or to feed Molly, Bella's black and white mouser. Best of all, Rosie liked to take the basket to the hen box at the side of the henhouse. She had to drag it, but would not allow anyone to help her. There she would lift the lid and take out the eggs, one at a time and, bent double over the rim of the basket, put them gently into the bottom.

Sometimes she had to wait until an egg was laid and the brown hen had left the nest, then the egg to harden before she could pick it up. "There's no fresher egg than that," Bella would say. "You might like it for your tea in an egg cup with bread and butter, Rosie. How's that?"

Chapter 7

There was the usual lull at the bakery now that Peter had loaded up the mended van and started his rounds. Sally was taking her time to ice and decorate a few plain buns and was lost in her thoughts when suddenly Jim Macaulay put his head round the door. He had walked down to see if they had a pie or two and a cake for his supper.

"I feel like a day off from wondering what to have and then cooking it for myself," he told Sally. "It's about time Pip and I had treats."

"Who's Pip?" asked Sally.

"He's my little black lurcher. You must have seen him about, though he keeps close to home and he's usually in his basket after he's been out with me," said Jim. He leaned in the doorway and watched her as she cleared away the icing bowl and rinsed it at the sink. He smiled to himself as he saw her slim figure moving neatly about the room as she put two pies and a walnut cake into a paper bag for him. The truth was, his meeting with her last Sunday and her delightful confusion as she regained her feet and composure after her heated tussle in the brambles had brought home to him his continuing loneliness since he'd lost Pat. Since he'd started to make a success of the Wooden Fender, he found more time to look up and take notice of his lonely state. He had relished the diversion that weekend. Trudging home afterwards to the quiet with just Pip's welcome from his basket, marked more than ever, Jim's lack of close human company. He had been more thoughtful than usual as he served the customers that evening.

She really was an attractive woman, he thought, and he was amused that time, after all, was having its healing effect.

Suddenly he felt uplifted that he could appreciate the sight of a pretty woman once more. Had an invisible barrier been lifted and set him free to look forward at last? "Oh, Pat," he breathed.

Sally looked up at him and asked, "Would you like some of this pie filling for Pip's supper? There's some sausage meat left too, if you'd like." She looked away again quickly as she caught his unguarded, intense look.

He stood up suddenly straighter and looked serious as the realisation dawned that he'd really visited the shop to see Sally again, not for the baking, and she always seemed to be glad to see him. That husband of hers was a surly great lump. Not his business to wonder how they got on, or whether she was happy, he told himself. Now he had sorted the job out and the place was running more smoothly, he had too much time on his hands. He'd better get back home and prepare the pub to open at lunchtime.

He wandered home in deep thought all the same, the bag of food she'd given him warm in his grasp.

Sally was thoughtful too, after he'd left. He was such a quiet man, almost self-effacing, but he looked so attractive when he smiled. He seemed to be quite the opposite of Peter with his forthright ways and his air of assuming that she would naturally obey his wishes. Well, she reminded herself, it was her fault as much as Peter's. She was going to have to get on and sort a few things out with him at last. Their marriage would have to be more of a partnership and he would have to ask her opinion sometimes rather than simply bulldozing her into doing things his way.

When Peter came in at midday for his dinner, he looked a bit askance at the meat pie she had warmed for him instead of the meat and two vegetables he was used to having, but he kept quiet for a change. He thought she was a bit unsteady lately and shied away from the uneasiness.

Sally didn't mention Jim had called that morning although she was still caught up with distracting thoughts of him. She knew there was a certain antipathy between the two

37

men. She, who had always been so guileless and open in her relationship with Peter, kept Jim's visit to herself – and added to the distance now between them.

Chapter 8

Jim often called now with the excuse that as he lived on his own he didn't want to bother cooking for himself as well as running a pub. Sally had noticed that he seemed to turn up when Peter was out on the rounds and guessed he looked across the field to see Peter go out in the van, before he visited. Certainly neither man had attempted to overcome their mutual dislike of one another. However, she found herself very much looking forward to seeing Jim – he was so cheerful and diverting. Sometimes he brought Pip with him and the little dog, at first very timid, was at last won over, though Sally didn't know whether it was her gentle persistence or her pasties which had done the trick. Since the two men avoided each other, she still omitted to mention Jim's visits to Peter. She was in bad enough straits with Peter at the moment without giving any reason for more discord. She would tell him when things were better.

Shortly after Peter had taken his awful van to a mechanic friend to be cobbled together yet again, Jim called round. "It's a beautiful morning, my lovely, and I want to show you a badger sett Pip and I found yesterday. It's along by the East orchards – can you come now?" Sally's small qualms were swept away, by his enthusiastic invitation. She and Peter had exchanged yet more heated words on the state of the van and why he persisted in carrying on with it instead of shelling out some of the money they had earned for a new one. Peter had gone off in a huff flinging back that it was his job to take care of this side of the business and not her worry. The van would be good for a few more miles yet. Sally couldn't have cared less about badgers at that moment, but just to get away from this moody old atmosphere – and with Jim!

They stole away across the field at the back of the bakery and through the gate into the orchards. She had gladly left the hot room full of cooling ovens without dressing warmly and now missed her coat. She should have thought to put it on. He saw her shiver in her short sleeved jumper. "Of course, you must be cold, my dear. I rushed you away without giving you time to think," and quite casually he put his arm round her. She started with alarm and made to move away but Jim's banal, "Chivalry isn't dead, Sally," and his grin, relaxed her and she gratefully snuggled against his side as they walked over the morning-wet grass.

As they moved quietly to a grass bank dividing this field from the next, Jim pointed out the surprisingly narrow oval entrance to the badger sett he'd come across yesterday. "Look, Sally, the sow's put her bedding out to air," Jim said softly, and Sally leaned forward, intrigued to see small, dry mounds of grass neatly sitting at the mouth of the sett. "It's a pity we can't come back in the evening and catch a glimpse of them scratching about," he added. "You can see badgers in the dark if you use a red piece of material across a torch beam. Well, that's what I read, anyway."

Not for the first time, Sally wondered, as she looked back and up at Jim how it was she had come to enjoy Jim's visits so much; now she did not hesitate to walk out alone with him like this. There was a very attractive self-containment about him, an air of comfortable quietness with himself and the world. She suspected that this sureness must have been hard-won, starting from the time he had lost Pat and taking him along the road to the Wooden Fender. She had looked forward more and more to his calls at the bakery and if, for some reason, he had not taken the path through the field to see her for a day or two, she would find herself watching and waiting, or standing in the yard staring across the space between their two houses, the washing still in the basket, and wondering why he had not come.

From those visits at the beginning when (she now admitted) they were both in some kind of loneliness, their

40

friendship had easily progressed to such outings as today. And why shouldn't she steal cheerful days for herself from an unhappy life?

Back again on her own in the bakery, she began to question her motives for being so happy with Jim more closely – then ducked away quickly. But not before she acknowledged that seeing this man and grasping those moments away from her crushed life at the bakery had become the highlight of her life.

Thereafter he would often call with a thinly disguised excuse for the two of them to walk across the fields beyond their premises – and they made sure to part before they were seen. Theirs was a small world whose inhabitants would be more than interested to see them too much together.

There came a time when he said: "I've never told you much about Pat, have I Sally, but we had a good marriage and it is only lately that I have begun to look forward again. I have said 'if only' so many times – it never helped."

"Dear Peter, I can't imagine how you coped with such a tragedy – I don't think I ever could! Do you still miss her very much?" she asked, a slight frown showing her concern as she turned against his arm, looking up, but his gaze was caught beyond her as he began to relive, as he related to her, the events of that terrible day.

"Pat wanted to shop that Saturday afternoon. She needed some material to cover an old chair of her mother's. I was going to turn the garden over while she was away, but it came on to rain. She picked up her umbrella, said she'd be back soon..." Jim paused at this. They had drawn together as he was speaking and now she held him closely as he recalled:

"I dug out my old seafaring binoculars and took myself off to the reservoir. I often used to go there at the weekends and watch the birds..." Jim stopped, uneasy and then in a rush, explained, "Pat was knocked over crossing the road. She tried to run across in the downpour to a shop and pulled her umbrella down as she ran. She didn't see the car, and it couldn't stop. The brakes in the wet..." Jim took a deep breath as if saying these few words had exhausted him, then realised that talking about it now, for the first time in more than four years, was easing his mind. Sally was quiet, willing him to continue.

"They said she'd jumped a puddle, waving that damned umbrella around. The driver stamped on his brakes, but the car skidded and slewed into her. And all the while I was watching birds. Useless! I strolled back home in the evening without a care – and there was a policeman waiting."

Sally was lost for words, her arms tightly round him, her head bent, until Jim, not talking now, gently grasped her shoulders until she lifted her face and with relief she watched him smile gently back at her.

Deliberately, quietly, he said, "But you turned my life around, Sally. Ever since I first saw you on the road in a tizzy that day... With you, just your company like this you make a simple walk the best thing in the day. When we part, it's the worst."

Suddenly, knowing that they were about to breach the scant barrier and tumble into the unknown, Sally felt unsure and quietly walked a pace or two away. Over the days and weeks of their meetings, she had become so close to him. It could no longer be borne to hug it to herself as a secret; wanting and wondering – where he was; what he was doing; if he was thinking of her – when he was out of her sight. And as Jim's hold on her happiness had grown, so she had drifted further away from Peter.

Worriedly, Jim caught her arm and turned her to look at him. "What is it? Have I upset you? Oh, Sally, I shouldn't have burdened you with all this, but it was really to tell you..."

"Yes, I know –"

"...that since I met you, since right at the start, I have realised that with you, only with you, I can –" Jim stopped, gathered an agitated breath, "We can be happy again. Sally, you know I love you, you must know."

"I'm married, Jim. Married," she said despairingly. "Though, God knows, that's just a piece of paper now. I want to be with you. All the time."

"Sally. Oh, Sally," Jim had both arms round her now hugging her, strong and close, the cool outdoor man-smell of him taking her last small resistance and leaving the only certainty; that she loved this man. She revelled in the delicious sensation of her bare arms against the rough weave of his coat as she deliberately slid her hands around his neck and, their faces close and drawing closer, they kissed with an intensity of feeling held so long in check, but now broken free and overwhelming.

He could not let her go. Sally stayed defenceless in the protective warmth of his arms until in a drawn moment of happiness belonging only to them, uncertainty slipped away, and the world went quiet.

Some time later, Sally stirred and wrapped her fingers round one of the strong hands still holding her so close. "Jim. Jim! We have to face up to it. There's Peter. How are we going to tell Peter? I can't stay living in the same house with him. I realise now he has always wanted to control me. He was clinging while I was backing away. Then I met you," and she turned and gave him a wistful little smile. They kissed, softly this time, acknowledging a loving commitment, but while Jim was content in knowing that he would do everything he could to support Sally when she faced Peter, Sally was wondering from where she would find the courage to face her husband.

"We must go back, Jim," she said reluctantly. "How can I tell Peter?"

"We'll do it together, Sally. We shall have to make plans to move away then, my darling. You realise, don't you, that we can't stay here?"

Chapter 9

On yet another Sunday morning in October, Bob Carden was checking the orchards to see if there was anything to be done or supplied before picking resumed on Monday morning. The Cox's apples were being harvested now towards the end of the year's crops and only the careful pickers were invited to help here. Some of the women earned a good deal more than others, but those pickers could be careless in their handling of the fruit. It was part of Bob's job to see that the fruit left the orchards in top condition to keep the Settlement's 'Foxash' brand in the forefront at Covent Garden.

He had left Bess and Mac at home this morning. Both had clamoured to come as soon as they saw Bob draw on his Wellingtons in the back shed. Mac whirled round in front of him and pushed his nose into Bob's face as he leaned forward to tuck his trousers into his boots, but Bess was in season and the dogs had to be separated this time. She was in the day kennel in the back garden, bouncing and barking in the run. Neither he nor Jean always wanted to have puppies under their feet and Bess would be all the stronger next time. Jean had distracted them with a bone each, which the butcher had included with this week's joint of beef when he'd called.

If there was one thing Bob really looked forward to, it was going home to a midday roast, particularly beef, after a walk on a glorious morning like this. He strode out, shotgun tucked under his arm, inspecting the trees from side to side as he went, in a way which had now become automatic. He found, to his satisfaction, that there were still a number of good apples to be harvested. The tall ladders were already arranged along the path nearest to the trees waiting to be picked. They were heavy, wooden things, and had to be dragged from tree to tree. There were three long poles one of which was crossed with steps leading to a small platform on top to take the baskets. These pickers were paid by the hour 'piece rates' to encourage easy, careful handling of these choicest Christmas apples to be put, unbruised, into cold storage.

The women certainly earned their money on this job, he thought, and with the young children back at school, they worked longer hours, too. He always turned a blind eye when pickers walked home with fruit-bulging bags which had held their lunchtime sandwiches and flasks, though there were always one or two who liked to try to take advantage, even to filling the bottom of a baby's pram with pounds of fruit and vegetables. He had to be seen to put a stop to that! He knew the women would be making jam and bottling fruit when they were home – a taste of bright summer and autumn days to help take them through winter.

Since all seemed in order, Bob finally gave himself time to enjoy the morning. A slanting gauze of mist rose through the trees, steadily evaporating as the sun climbed. His feet felt pleasantly cool, even in his Wellingtons, from the dew-soaked grass, and he gave a small shiver, more in anticipation of a warmer day to come than in an acknowledgement of the lingering cold. Then, rabbits being off the menu now, he was wondering if there were any hare, or even a partridge or two, he could bag as a bonus on the day, when he saw the movement of two people leaning closely together. They were a good distance along the row of trees he was crossing. Jim turned towards them and started, ready to call out, just as the sun heaved itself higher to scatter the final wisps of mist, but the stance of them made him stop. It was his Sally and that Jim Macaulay and they were in more than earnest conversation if the body language was anything to go by. What the hell was going on? Puzzled, and with instinctive caution, he backed away. He needed time to think, and rare intuition guided him to retreat before he was seen. With a last glance in their direction, to see him holding her across the shoulders – and she not backing away, by God, or he'd have been across there so fast – he hefted his gunstock tightly under his arm and strode back to the Land rover.

He felt very much at odds with himself now, his morning ruined in some indefinable way. Surely his daughter wasn't seeing that man, surely not! He was glad they were too engrossed to catch a glimpse of him through the trees. He didn't know how to cope with this. He'd find out what Jean had to say about it.

Chapter 10

Peter, back at the bakery, relayed the invitation from Jean that they go to have tea with her next Sunday. "Your Mum says she's not seen you for ages – what do you think? In fact, I was going to suggest that you might like to go on your own, if I run you over in the van. You know how you hate the Sunday evening bookwork and it would give me a chance to get it up to date while you were out and you could have a good 'girl' talk with your mother at the same time."

Sally, with her world turned nearly upside down, was relieved to fall in with this suggestion straight away. It was out of the question that she wouldn't go, but her conscience made her wonder if her mother had heard anything untoward about her 'friendship' with Jim. She would have found the strain of sitting across from a discerning mother while trying to play happy families with Peter close by too nerve-wracking to bear. As it was, it would certainly be a blessing to be away from her home – and Peter – for a relaxing evening with her mother, and unwind from the underlying tension that now dogged her every waking moment. "Well, if you're sure you won't mind, I'll do that then," Sally said on a sigh. "Will you tell Mum when you call on Thursday please, Peter? I'm sure she won't mind your not going when you explain about doing the books."

Jean had plenty on her mind on Sunday while getting the tea together for Sally who was due to arrive soon. Setting a pretty table for them both was something Jean had always enjoyed when Sally (usually with Peter) called for a rare Sunday tea. It made a little occasion for them to be served cakes, looking tempting on pretty china, that they themselves hadn't baked. She put some cooled cheese straws on a doily and cut bread to make sandwiches. She wished she had something a bit more special than Spam to put between the slices, but the new margarine just out on Mrs Brown's shelves went a good way to help the filling, as did her red tomato chutney which she added knowing how fond of it Sally had always been. She had used what was left of her small butter reserve to put buttercream in the sponge she'd made that morning and stood deep in thought while spooning her home-made raspberry jam into the sponge as well. Like all the housewives at this time of year, she was saving as much dried fruit as she could towards her Christmas cake, so fruit cakes were now very rarely on her tea table. Hers would not be a 'shouting cake' if she could help it (so called because the thin sprinkling of currants therein were so lonely it was said that they started calling to one another). It wasn't often she and Sally had the chance to have a get-together and she was very much looking forward to spoiling her with a good tea and having a long engaging chat. She was just bent double while getting her good china out of the sideboard on which stood a disgruntled-looking row of Toby jugs, when Bob loped in with the two eager Labradors in tow, straight from his orchard rounds and on to her swept carpet.

"Robert Carden, get those looney great dogs out of here now!" she directed without turning her head. "I've just this minute cleared up the last lot, and Sally is due any moment."

Bob backtracked hastily, the dogs, tails down now, all but tripping him up. At the door, he turned round and asked "Look, love, would you like me to take these hounds off for a decent walk while you and Sally have the place to yourselves? They've been in the Land Rover with me and they're feeling a bit cooped up. I reckon they need to have a bit of a run. I can have my tea later on my own."

Setting the cups and plates down on the little table by the window, she turned to him gratefully and said: "That's the best suggestion you've made today, old lad," and more quietly, "Thanks a lot, dear." Neither of them had forgotten for one moment what he'd told her he'd seen in the orchard two weeks ago. Jean had been brooding on it and what to do ever since. She felt she could just about manage to tread carefully through what might turn out to be a small minefield on her own without wondering what Bob would come out with if things went haywire. Or, best of all, Sally might need to confide in her mother without a man putting a clumsy oar in.

She jumped when Sally and Peter gave a peremptory knock on the front door and pushed it open knowing it was left on the latch for them. Sally bounced in followed by the always slower Peter who gave Jean a swift greeting before saying he'd be back later, say around 8 p.m. for Sally and quickly left them to it.

Jean, happy to have her daughter to herself for once, forgot her worries long enough to give her a welcome peck on the cheek and unravel her from her coat and scarf. She took them into the kitchen to leave across a chair. While she put the kettle on the gas she called, "I've been so looking forward to this. How are you then, and Peter?" Sally, bending down to take off her outdoor shoes, was glad her mother couldn't see her face when she said "Very well, thanks Mum, and Peter the same. Busy, of course – as always!"

"Keeps you out of mischief, then," and Jean could have bitten off her tongue. Why was it that, as soon as something should not be mentioned or alluded to, it would always pop out to cause trouble? She was being too sensitive, of course. She went back to the table with the teapot ensconced in a blue tea cosy and smiled innocently at Sally. Sally followed her to the table set with a crisp white cloth and the willow pattern china she remembered from when she was a small child. Jean, an excellent gardener, had found some rust-coloured chrysanthemums before the frosts would turn them black and put them on the windowsill in the cut-glass jug her mother had left to her.

Jean settled herself in one of the tall backed dining chairs and passing Sally a cup said, "Do you know where they are having the Guy Fawkes bonfire this year? Bella said she hoped they weren't going to burn all the broken old chip baskets like they did last year outside their house. She was quite sure it was dangerous and would burn her house down if the wind veered round! You could see the blaze for miles."

On safe ground, Sally sat back with a semblance of contentment. "Peter saw the children putting some wood and rubbish on a heap outside the packing shed earlier this week, but apparently Bowles had to ask the men to shift it further away from the sheds before they came back and put more on. Still, I think they plan to carry on with it where it now is. Did you think of going along, Mum?"

"Oh, no, I hate the things, and we stay in with the wireless on loudly for Bess and Mac. Mac barks at anything he doesn't understand – he wants to get out there when he hears the bangs, but Bess would rather it all went away. They're used to shotgun noise, of course, but they can't fathom firework noises." Jean leant forward to pass the plate of sandwiches to Sally, and didn't mention that she thought her daughter was looking a bit pale and washed out. She'd lost weight too.

"I do like to see the fireworks though. I generally go outside to stand and watch them, but they're soon over, aren't they. Jim says–" and Sally broke off, red colour spreading across her face. Having Jim in the back of her mind all the time and now beginning to relax and talk socially, especially to her mother, it would have been a miracle if she hadn't let his name slip.

"Jim, Jim who?" asked Jean feigning unconcern.

"Oh, Jim Macaulay, he calls in from time to time – our neighbour at the Wooden Fender," Sally tried to sound light and offhand. "He has a lurcher, and you speaking about dogs made me..." Sally looked up at her mother who was watching her quietly. "You know, don't you Mum," was said as a statement, then Sally looked down at her lap, her hair hiding her face. There were times when Sally was growing up that she thought her mother must be a witch, she seemed to guess so much that Sally wanted to keep secret. Her mother had jokingly told her once never to play poker with anybody (what was 'poker' she had wondered at the time) as her face always gave her away.

"There's a lot I don't know," replied her mother, troubled. "What is it my love?"

"Peter and I haven't been getting along for quite a while now. I feel – have felt for a long time – that he seems to need me more for the work I do in that wretched bakery than as a wife – Mum, any woman would please him if she worked like I did putting loaves in, loaves out of those ovens all day!"

Jean, at first inclined to laugh at such a notion, saw Sally's serious expression and said, "But you were always the pigeon pair, and if ever a couple were set for life it seemed to be you two. Life never was one continual round of excitement, you know, and you have been married for a few years now."

"We had hardly any time together before he went off to serve in the War. All those years away when his parents helped me in the bakery and I was just longing for him to come home! And then when he did well, he seemed to be so morose – didn't want to speak and needed to be on his own and after all the time I waited just for him to come back. It was all I lived for!" All her pent-up feeling was pouring out now, a long-needed release and Jean sat without moving, letting her speak.

"You know how he was to start with after all that time away, and we all thought he'd get to grips with it and come round – you said wait a bit, Mum. I did my best, I truly did. I knew he needed me to be there so I tried to be cheerful and wait, until it became a routine, he sullen, and me, just trying to appease him. It was all wrong; so unfair to us both!" And she groped for the handkerchief in her sleeve.

"And now it's become more than that. Peter and I have grown away from one another. He's wedded to his work, it's his life, and I can't see an end to it, or a real purpose in it any more. Yes, it was all we both wanted at the start, but it is taken for granted that I get on with it and do everything he says, that we don't go out or get away from the place for even a day. I am stuck in a rut and I can see no end to it. We are

51

older now, I know, grown up. All the fun went out of our lives with the war years. Well, I hardly saw him. Despite all we tried to do to mend things when he came home, the happiness never really came back. I can't – don't want to – go through the rest of my life like this." And in a smaller, wistful voice, "I might have stuck it out if a family had come along. I shall never know. I would have liked a family."

Instantly Jean picked up on that. Of all things, she and Bob would have loved grandchildren and she had hinted to Sally about this in her and Peter's early marriage, to be met with an airy, "There's plenty of time for children," from her daughter. Now Jean asked, "Was there a reason, dear, that you didn't?"

"Not that either of us know of, but then again, I have realised that Peter isn't a bit interested and I feel that may be because he wants always to be the centre of my attention and for me to be bound, like him, hand and foot to the business without the distraction of a baby about the place. When I've broached the subject, he's always been non-committal, till now I don't think it's even a good idea – it wouldn't work if he was set against it. If he wasn't happy, he'd make sure I wouldn't be." Sally sat back, her food untouched, the mood in the room as darkening now as the last rays of the sun cutting across the flat Essex field beyond the window.

Jean was stunned that things had got this far. "That's a bitter thing to say, Sally. Of all the couples I know, I felt you two were of one mind about each other and that it would last. And where does Jim Macaulay come into all this?" she asked with some asperity. Where do you get these ideas from, these notions that the grass is greener..." All the old saws flitted unbidden through her mind. 'You reap what you sew', or 'you make your bed and you lie on it', this last always trotted out when there was marital discord.

"He has been calling for weeks now, off and on, and seems to have enjoyed my company as much as I have enjoyed talking to him. He takes an interest in me–my life and..."

"You know where that will lead to my girl, don't you!" cut in Jean, her voice hardening, "or has it already?" Bob was right in his interpretation of when he saw them together in the orchard.

"Oh, Mum," from Sally told Jean that all her fears were justified.

She tried, "Can't you be content with what you've got? A (so far as we know) faithful husband who provides for you, doesn't drink – be thankful for it!"

Goaded, Sally raised her voice as she replied, "A husband who sees me as an unpaid skivvy, to be ordered about, whose approval I feel I have to earn each day, with never a compliment or a cuddle, or a suggestion of a day out, carrying on just as he always has all his life, getting his own way! And then along comes a man who smiles and listens to me as if I really do have something interesting to say, who makes me feel wanted and attractive just by looking at me – oh, I'm sure you don't want to hear all this. But the fact is, we have grown very close, very close," she repeated at a whisper.

The tea had gone cold in the pot, the daylight had gone from the room but each woman sat sadly in her chair, unmoving, regrouping her thoughts, neither thinking to put the light on.

"Well," said Jean eventually, rousing herself, trying to understand her unhappy daughter. "Why have you kept this to yourself for all this time, dear? I knew things were not quite so happy with you lately, but we all have our awkward times in marriage."

"I kept hoping Peter would get over the war and get better, be his old self again, that time would do the trick." Sally didn't add that she thought her parent's rigid outlook on keeping their marriage vows would colour their opinion and make her feel inadequate. She, too, had heard the one where you made your bed and you lay on it.

Jean put more coal on the dying fire and sat with her hands out to it, suddenly shivering, her face looked older with the deep sadness she now felt. Sally crept to the chair the other side of the fire as Jean said, "I had you just after the First World War and all your father and I wanted then was for a 'normal', uneventful life, with regular work for him and enough to feed and clothe us all. We were grateful to be free of that War and worked hard to get on our feet with our family growing up, and that's how it's always been; and through the next war, too. My mother always said we had to keep within our station in life and to know our place, whatever that was, but I never believed in tripe like that. I preferred the one where 'God helped those who helped themselves.' It certainly made more sense. Each generation is different – has to be – but woe betide you, my girl, if this comes to leaving your husband. The very few divorces I've known about as I've gone through life are very painful experiences for both parties, and you know, incidentally, that you'd never be able to take a penny or a stick of furniture for yourself. All you have worked for will belong to Peter, of course. Have you thought this through? Oh, Sally, I don't think you have! Can't you talk to him?"

Sadly, Sally realised that she and her mother were far apart when it came down to their outlook on life, the division of two generations. She still didn't think her mother had guessed how far things had got, to the point where she was now in love with Jim and he with her, and that sooner or later she would have to face Peter and then the fat would be in the fire. Well, at least today she'd made it clear to her mother the way things were going. It should prepare her and her father a little more for when things got worse – and they would have to if she were ever to get free of Peter. Her feet felt like lead as she got up finally and walked across the room to the light switch.

Bob, who had seen Jean and Sally in deep conversation as he'd passed the side window with the two muddy dogs, had hosed them down gently and dried them off, had switched the lamp on in the shed and fallen to his ongoing job of sorting all the bits out until the great day when his shed would finally be tidy. He could see things didn't look very happy indoors.

Later, as he watched Jean brush invisible crumbs with the side of her hand from the pristine cloth before putting the crockery quietly on the tray to take to the kitchen, he tried to comfort her.

"It has to be her life, Jean. I am as appalled as you and just as sorry that things have got this far. Honestly, dear, there is nothing you or I can do – she has to find out for herself."

She wondered if it would have been a different story if Sally had had children. She has no patience with some of her friends who declared that a marriage wasn't a marriage without children; what rubbish, and where did it leave devoted couples who, for one reason or another, couldn't have children?

She added tears to the water as she slowly washed up her blue tea set.

Chapter 11

"Not tired again?" Peter asked later, exasperated as Sally turned away from him in bed for the second time in a row. This was a rum do. There were precious few home comforts today and no mistake. First, he'd had to put up with a scratch meal and now this! What was the matter with her lately? He was a good husband, heaven knew. He gave her a good home and she had no money worries like some he knew. He didn't drink or stray, though he could have chanced his luck on some of the late bakery rounds when there were women alone at home. There was that Trixie Langham, she'd been widowed these past – how many years? Lived on her own for all of them, well except for that menagerie she gave a home to. Lying awake, restless, he went off on a reverie fuelled by resentment while Sally slept with seeming unconcern by his side.

He bet Trixie was the right side of forty and still an attractive woman. Did Sally think he was made of stone? He had tried a few passes when he'd knocked at her door with bread on his late-night round: "It's so cold, love, you feel my hands!" to be met with, "You can keep your hands to yourself, Peter Starling!" but said with an arch smile and the offer of a cup of tea, which he'd reluctantly declined. He was sure she thought he was one good-looking man and only the thought of Sally had kept him on the straight and narrow. He knew some men might have thought him pretty stupid, when the woman seemed so willing. If only Sally knew! Would she even care? He turned over restlessly and Sally stirred but only to move further away, pulling herself into a tight ball and taking the covers with her.

Peter had had things his own way since he could

remember. His parents doted on their only child and whatever he wanted seemed to have materialised the whole time he was growing up. Then Sally had simply carried on where they had left off – she had adored him from the start and so, of course, he'd never had to try too hard to please her. He had been the oldest in the class and she one of the youngest. He had been big for his age although surprisingly, considering all the cooked pies and cakes he had always had access to at home, not fat. His voice had broken before the other boys in his class and this had been a great embarrassment to him. He'd had to start shaving before he left school. A lot of the girls had admired him and Sally was flattered when he'd asked her out. 'Smitten' was the word. He had always been so sure of her and had never questioned her loyalty. Was that why she had said he was taking her for granted?

Things had changed in the six or so years he'd been back from the War. The Army had practically pounced on him in the beginning, a strong, ex–National Service man, just the right age for call-up, who knew how to bake. Home many times had they told him that the Army marched on its stomach? And so he'd spent the entire War catering for the troops in the canteens and, like all his comrades, seen sights he'd rather have forgotten, and certainly had never wanted to speak about to anyone, let alone his Sally. He had simply wanted to get home and start afresh, leaving all the War memories behind him.

In the beginning, she had asked him from time to time what was wrong, when predictably his involuntary recall of bloody battles and thoughts of fallen comrades had got him down. No matter how hard he tried to put those dreadful years behind him, inevitably there were days of deep sadness. He had dealt with it by withdrawing into himself, bottling it up instead of pouring it out like a weak idiot and upsetting her. Sally's forced brightness had sometimes served to heighten his lonely despondency, but he felt his only recourse was to present a strong, silent front until his dark moods lightened again. Least said, soonest mended, he hoped, and in the last year or two he had felt happier. Anyway, he was older now, and bound to be more sober with his bread-winning responsibilities.

He shifted again, irritably. They were just going through a bad patch, that was all. All marriages did from time to time, he was sure. They'd just been a bit unlucky lately, he supposed. He determined to buy her a bunch of flowers from one of the smallholdings tomorrow. Women were extraordinarily pleased with a bunch of flowers. One or two of the neighbours left cut chrysanths out by their gates this time of the year. He'd see when he was out on the rounds in the morning. It was a pity there was no one to leave to carry on the baking while they took a holiday somewhere, he thought. Who on earth did he know who could begin to take over the job? No, it couldn't be done and he didn't know any other job either. You don't change horses in mid-stream, he said to himself and what's more he enjoyed being his own boss, not cooped up in a factory somewhere clocking on and off. No, he'd have to carry on the way he was and wait for the hiccup to pass!

Chapter 12

Trixie Langham would have been very amused if she'd known of Peter's fantasy concerning her, as he lay in bed, awake and miserable, by his wife's side. She would not have considered herself to be the subject of any man's interest since her life with Walter.

She was sitting now at midday beside the fire to warm herself before the afternoon chores outside. Picking up the bowl of hot soup before Inky, a cat's whisker away, got there first, she began to reminisce.

Eight years ago, when the War ended and Walter was discharged with a wound and a small pension, she had, with relief, left the hurly burly of a fast assembly line in a munitions factory. They had put their old lives behind them and started anew on a smallholding along Hunting Lane with the Land Settlement Association.

For Trixie this was a dream come true. She had hankered to be a land girl to fulfil her role in the war effort but, living in London with her parents, while Walter was abroad in the Army, she had found herself in a factory with older women and 'just marrieds' like herself. There were only so many land girls needed and most of them had country backgrounds, which made them instantly more useful.

At last they had a place of their own. She and Walter worked side by side with huge will and enthusiasm to get their piece of land producing. They were interested enough to take advice from wherever it came, as long as they could see it would work. They were not the only ones in the neighbourhood starting to grow vegetables and keep farm animals and advice was sorely needed. The Land Settlement had many experienced managers to choose from, where individual farms had foundered at that time and left farming generations in a slump, without hope.

At the end of Hunting Lane, they were somewhat out of the mainstream of activity along the main road, but enthralled as they were with this new, and to them freer, life, they worked long hours without distraction. When Walter's leg ached he would take himself off to the greenhouse to prick out the tomato plants where he could stand straight, or add up the books; there was always some job he could do to pull his weight. Trixie, fit and happy, would carry on being the mainstay until Walter's leg, which he could not bend since the knee wound, eased again.

They were allotted as many weaner piglets as they wanted or could accommodate in the piggery at the top of the garden part of their holding. These they fattened and returned to the centre collection point which housed the offices and packing shed with the lorry park alongside. Trixie was always much more interested in keeping animals than growing vegetables and soon acquired two white kid goats to bring on until she could take them to the billy goat. When they kidded, she passed on the kids to a neighbour and sold the milk from the nannies to the centre, trading the odd pint or two for someone else's surplus produce. There were the pigs, goats, the inevitable chickens and a good mouser who preferred to live independently outside, but for whose kittens she was always having to find homes. With all these animals concentrating her maternal instincts and, with Walter usually in shouting distance, she felt that, at long last her life was happy and fulfilled. Walter was content to tend his tomatoes and plant out the mixed vegetables and rows of flowers to cut. He would look up when Trixie bolted past hanging on grimly to the chain of one or the other of the goats to peg out to graze or bent double with a wide square board in her hands, drove a sow with new piglets to a fenced off clover patch and felt he had the best of the bargain. There was still a lot of the child in Trixie which he found very engaging, and sent him cheerfully about his chores. He wasn't so happy

60

about the young jackdaw she had been given by one of the boys who talked to them sometimes when they passed the gate. She would carry the thing around on her shoulder and had taught him to say "Hallo Jack", which he had teased here was highly original. Jack was a very possessive bird and resented Walter's coming anywhere he thought might be too near Trixie and squawked warningly, shifting agitatedly on Trixie's shoulder. Walter had offered to wring 'the spiv's' neck more than once, and would be glad when that particular bird had fallen off his perch, but one look at Trixie told him, if he ever needed to confirm it, that she was in her element looking after all the livestock. He just hoped there wouldn't be too many pet animals here not earning their keep.

Then there they were, in 1947, three years after starting their smallholding; it had become one of the most productive on the Land Settlement.

That year of 1947 would be the year remembered as one of the coldest, most biting winters anyone could recall. It went on and on, freezing the whole country it seemed, forever.

Farm workers, used to following the vagaries of the weather all year round were hard put to carry on. Trixie and Walter, working side by side, wrenched at the Brussels sprouts in the deep frozen outdoors until their fingers stopped working, stiff with cold, while the vegetables still clung solidly to the stems. Water for the animals had to be fetched from indoors, every bucketful, the taps outside, along with everything else, were frozen up. There was a narrow line between keeping the house warm enough and running out of coal, in case the delivery lorries couldn't get through to renew stocks – everyday living, in fact, was a struggle to survive for everyone.

Nothing lasts forever, not even the winter of 1947. By extraordinary contrast, this winter was followed by one of the hottest summers most had experienced.

That was the year when the fields of hay ripened together, the seed heads came early and the areas between the semi-detached blocks of houses were ready for harvesting all at once. If there was any complaint, it would have been that the lack of rain made the grass sparse and patchy but, not knowing how the weather would hold, everyone who could or would help out were welcomed to get the hay in off the fields.

With his early planting done, and Trixie more than happy to hurtle energetically around 'from pig to goat' as Walter put it, he volunteered, a thing he said he'd never done in the Army, and so found himself on his way to help with the hay harvest. He wheeled his bicycle to the front of the house. The bicycle repair man had adapted it with a fixed peg on one side for his straight leg to rest, allowing his good leg to do the work. Trixie looked up from mixing pig swill and, taking a piece of string from her bib pocket, tied her hair back from her hot face. He turned to call that he'd be back by midday if he could, but not to worry if they were too busy and she gaily waved him off, a small compact figure neat in boiler suit trousers at a time when every woman wore skirts, notwithstanding they had seen the practicality of women during the war wearing trousers at their service jobs.

Walter was feeling his leg by late morning when they all stopped for water and to cool down. He poured a bottle of water over his head and shoulders and said nothing. All the men were far too hot to want to talk anyway, but sank down by the stacked hay, grateful for the short break. He was unused to this hard, heavy ongoing labour without much respite and would be glad when midday came and he could cycle home for an hour or so. He didn't feel much like eating, it was too hot, but would be relieved to sink down into his chair for a longer rest. Stacking hay was more involved, he'd found, than just hurling bales up onto the tractor trailer and hoping they'd land in the right place. Edgar, driving the Ferguson one minute and putting him right the next, had his own work cut out to cope in the heat, but they would soon finish clearing this field and he wanted to complete it before the midday break.

Edgar drove the last load through the five-bar gate across the track spanning a narrow, deep ditch onto the road. The trailer-load shook down, moving the bales, settling and unsettling as the trailer passed the gate posts. Walter stood wearily at the side resting his aching leg ready to shut the gate across with wry ceremony for a job well-done.

Just as Edgar turned the Ferguson onto the narrow road home, the nearside wheel of the two-wheeled flat trailer caught in the corner of the ditch and the nearest bales started to slide sideways, catching Walter with full force as they fell. There was an instant when Walter's shocked face was raised to see the oncoming bales, but then he was lost, knocked into the ditch with the heavy load massed on top of him. It was doubtful that even if he had been nimble on both feet, he could have managed to evade the falling bales and get clear of the ditch.

Calling frantically, first to Walter, then anyone who could help, Edgar fell into the ditch to pull off the bales until his rough hands bled. When they found Walter, it was too late; he had died where he had fallen, crushed under the weight of most of the load.

Frozen in shock, Trixie could not cry. Walter had been torn away from a happy, unfinished life and had left Trixie stunned, holding the painful, ragged edges of a deep wound which would be long and slow to heal.

She had lain in bed the day after the tragedy in disbelief that Walter was no longer there. She listened, then sprang out of bed in the certain knowledge that he was in the kitchen – he'd gone to make them tea before they set to outside. The sun was just rising but she could not take in that Walter wasn't there to see it. She made some tea but could not eat a thing; there was a huge lump in her throat that food could not pass. As she opened the back door to flood the kitchen with some life-giving sunshine, Inky, then a lively young tom cat, stalked in grandly, tail in air, with a small dead rat neatly laid across his jaws. He dropped it at her feet and sat back gazing up expectantly with wide green eyes. Blindly, Trixie walked straight past him and out to what she and Walter had called 'the small room', defining for them the more primitive way of life she and Walter had adjusted to along with the rest since leaving London. Inky was outraged. He didn't give all his treasures away, but the sixth sense which most pet cats have had prompted him on this occasion. He yowled the 'caterwaul' much like the barn cat calling her kittens to a kill but, getting no reaction, huddled down on the kitchen floor to eat the rat, his ears back listening for Trixie to return, when he'd have to pick it up smartly and run outside before she caught him.

Jack turned one wicked-looking black eye to Trixie who had reached his wire cage on top of the coat bunker and shrieked "Hallo Jack!" His harsh reveille brought her slowly out of her preoccupied thoughts again to unreal consciousness. She would be in shock for a long time.

The first thing that Trixie learned that morning was that her life would not stay where Walter had left her even though that was what she wanted. The complaining, hungry animals gave her no choice but to get started as always, feeding the livestock first and tending to their needs. Then she began looking towards Walter's chores such as watering the tomatoes in the greenhouse before the sun dried them out completely, but when she opened the greenhouse door, she became overwhelmed with an acute sense that she was invading Walter's territory and that he would not approve if she watered them too much, too little. No, it was too soon. She stepped quickly out and shut the glass door. She wished there were near neighbours now, from whom she could ask advice and would take the loneliness away just for a short while, but her nearest contact was when George Springett cycled up the lane to put Hector and Fancy out in the field. He didn't need to go as far as past her gate.

Later that day Mr Bowles stopped the Land rover outside and came diffidently up the path to offer condolences (not an industrial injury pension – such ideas were for the far future) to find her, face set, struggling with the watering. He set to,

64

helping her there and then and asked her to promise to call into 'Foxash' with any queries or worries she might have, and told her that he would always send one of the workmen with heavy machinery to help her, if needed. He left with the assurance that she could stay on in the tied house so long as she felt able to carry on doing the job on her own and felt it was the best he could offer her. He assuaged his unquiet mind with the thought that Walter should have known better than to stand so close to the heaving trailer – but then he was only four years out from London and was still learning. The locals brought up to rural life imbibed a respect for potentially dangerous animals and machinery as they went along. Even so, there were bad accidents from time to time. They were the worst part of farming life.

In the lonely days and weeks that followed, Trixie found she was a little less miserable outside in the sunshine with the animals than indoors and was grateful for the continuing warm weather which helped her with her tasks. Elsie called in now and then in the early days, once bringing her a fruit cake with, "I was just mixing a cake for my two, so I thought I'd make a bit extra for you, as I was calling by." Trixie was always pleased to see her and knew Elsie was hard put to go anywhere very far with Barry well on the way at that time, much less could she casually call by. Trixie was too far along the lane in her isolated home.

"There's something you may find very strange," she said to Elsie on one occasion, "but I don't ride a bike! My parents would not let me scoot about London on a cycle while I was growing up because of the traffic and, of course, we could get about where we wanted, more or less." Elsie immediately offered her old bicycle, updated with new three-speed gears. "I shan't be needing it for quite a little while," she said, patting her round front.

"Well, the truth is, whenever I've had the chance here to learn to ride a bicycle, I've made such a hash of it, and now I'm three years off forty, middle-aged for heaven sake, I don't think I can start to learn to balance. When Walter was here he did all the shopping and brought it home on his old bike." (She looked down and away as she said his name). "I've taken ages to walk to the shop and then haven't been able to get all I need because of lugging it home. There was so much Walter did that I'm a bit stretched to cope… " Trixie smiled to try to look cheerful although she'd trailed off.

"Leave that to me," said Elsie with decision. "Mr Brown calls with my stuff on the trade bike, since I'm grounded and Alan is away on that lorry of his. I'll ask him to take your order and bring it up. Give me a list, love, and I'll take it with me."

"Oh, that is so good of you, and another problem solved," answered Trixie gratefully.

Benny the Postman bringing the post passed back and forth on his rounds and gave her a call and a wave. From time to time he would stop to ask if she needed a hand with anything, and would often take the other end of something heavy she was lifting when he happened to call in or go past with the post. He bumped into George going up Hunting Lane to his beloved horses. "How's that young gal?" George asked him, puffing along on his rusty old bike. "I catch a glimpse of her now and then over the hedge when I bring the old horses back from the top end and she seems to be working her guts out. Do you reckon she'll stay?"

"I've never heard her say she's quitting," answered Benny, "and I think she's working out her demons, if you ask me. She doesn't get any fatter though!"

"Poor old Walter, went through all that in the War and then gets hisself killed three years after!" said George disgustedly, as if Walter should have been more careful. "It just don't seem right."

Trixie put down some food for Inky when she came indoors at midday. He stalked to his dish and delicately sniffed round the edge. There were still no tasty little morsels which used to appear to tickle his appetite, nor any interesting cooking smells lately, so he settled to eat what there was and drink some goats milk for which he had developed a taste since he was a kitten. Watching him lap steadily round the dish of milk, Trixie poured a glass for herself. Cooking and trying to eat a meal on her own was just too much bother. She took Jack on her shoulder sometimes for company as she went back and forth, though he nearly deafened her with his squawks. She would have to teach him a few more words or "Hallo Jack" would drive her mad.

Outside, doggedly working on autopilot, her mind elsewhere, she moved from one task to the other until light faded and she came in to the empty house drained of energy. Exhausted as she was and driving herself as she did, Trixie still couldn't sleep more than a few hours at a time. She didn't know if she was winning or not but, coming as a sudden revelation to her, was the thought that at no time had she even thought of giving up her little 'farm'. Feeling needed, that no one else could look after her charges the way she did, gave her a purpose, a reason to carry on. She found it amazing that Walter couldn't know what she was doing now. It would take an age to sink in that he wouldn't be back – still unbelievable! Weathering these low days, gave her a certain confidence that she was coping. Creeping through from that came the knowledge that she could cope on her own – was coping on her own.

September 1947 and looking round one hazy morning at what to do next, it dawned on her that she had achieved a good deal these past few months. She had grown on the majority of Walter's tomatoes, picking them daily to be collected for the packing shed. The sixteen piglets sparked out in the early autumn sunshine were growing fast in the care of the good Saddleback sow; she'd got that right, then crossed her fingers for the rest of it, the runner beans, marrows and the very last of the potatoes. The unthinkable had happened – she could never have contemplated starting this venture without Walter but, faced with the inevitable, she had given it her best. She had sent vegetables, planted in the spring by Walter, to market and the tomatoes had carried her through to the autumn crops.

As she took stock for what she had achieved these last few difficult months, there came stealing into her mind an inkling of pride. She was aware of a slowing down to a less frantic pace and the beginnings of some sense of satisfaction. Inky appeared at her feet, curling his blue-black tail round her legs as he paraded close in front of her. She bent to stroke his head and he purred as he lifted his front feet off the ground to make contact with her hand. In a rare burst of affection he allowed her to pick him up and carry him indoors to sit for a while on her lap, and for the first time since the dreadful day in June, she started to relax. With a sigh, she sat back and stroked the cat.

George called in next morning with a basket strapped across his bicycle carrier. His wife had given him a casserole dish of beef to take to her. George and his wife believed in eating heartily to fuel them for a physically active day, cold outside or not. She knew Trixie would not cook much on her own, let alone a meal which took so long in the oven.

"How's it going then?" George asked awkwardly, as he handed the dish to Trixie.

"I think I might be getting there, George." She smiled at him gratefully. "I do feel cut off sometimes though, and to walk anywhere after all the chasing around I do here, seems such an effort. I shall simply have to learn to ride a bicycle if I ever want to go to the village for much shopping, but my balance seems to go haywire whenever I try. I can't understand it."

She turned and took the casserole indoors and lifted the lid for a peep. It smelled rich and savoury. Inky appeared from she-never-knew-where and looked up with interest. "Yes, I know you old devil, this is more like it as far as you're concerned, isn't it?" and putting the dish in the larder cupboard, she went to show George round the smallholding and to ask his opinion on one or two things.

George followed slowly round and seemed impressed with all she was doing. Finally, as he reached his old bicycle again he seemed to make up his mind to say, "You've made a

damn good job of it all. Walter would be proud of you gal!"
And that did make Trixie cry. George stood quietly, looking
helplessly from left to right, waiting for Trixie to come out of
it.

He made another decision: "I can see you don't get much
freedom to leave the place though, having to walk
everywhere – no bike to help you out. What about getting
yourself a pony and trap?"

She stood transfixed. "What an idea!" The notion
enchanted her. "But, I haven't the first idea, George. What to
do, how to go about it – oh, I think it would be the perfect
answer, if I could do it!" Her face had come alive at the
thought, a smile eclipsing the dark in her eyes.

"Just an idea, but if you think it might be right for you,
I'll tell you the rest. There's a trap and all the trimmings, laid
up by the two wagons in the shed next to the horse stalls. It's
been on the estate since before Bowles's time. Beatrice, old
Harding's wife, used to fancy herself driving around in it, till
that little devil of a pony backed her into a ditch. He knew
she was nervous with him. It frightened Beatie so much (only
we had to call her Beatrice or she'd have one of her haughty
turns – barmy we thought) that she got out and left the lot –
walked home, and Edgar and I had to go and fetch poor old
Ted and the trap." George looked disgusted as he thought
about it. "We put the trap in the shed – and there it's stayed."

It hadn't been put quite like this at the time it happened
as George described it to Philbert Wright in the Wooden
Fender with much relish. "What do you think that old
Beatie's been and gone and done now!" he greeted Philbert,
who was leaning one elbow on the bar, pipe in hand.
"Harding went and left her in the trap while he called on a
tenant and that old Ted went and backed her arse over 'ead
into the ditch!" Philbert spluttered gleefully into his pint. The
Hardings were generally regarded as far too high and mighty
with grand ideas and too little knowledge of land
management to sit well with the tenants. "She righted herself
from hat to bustle and headed off home. Left old Ted stuck

on the end of the trap with his wheels in the ditch. That cut his gallop! I told 'em Ted were too much for 'em but they weren't listenin'."

"Always went at it like damn fools." Philbert gave his opinion.

"By the time Harding got back to where he'd left the wife, there weren't a particle of the missus, jus' Ted standing there looking daft. I had to take Edgar to give me a hand and get the trap back. They say they won't go out in it again." George moved to take his usual from the barman. Both men stood thoughtfully for a while, then, together, contentedly swallowed their beers.

"What about a pony, George? Where would that come from?" Trixie's mind flew ahead to all the possibilities while the idea took root.

"Ponies are easier to come by than traps, and cost a lot less," said George wisely. "There'll be one for you for sure, if I ask about. You be getting a bit o' shed clear and I'll let you know – it may take a while. We can get that trap clean and checked while we wait."

Watching him turn to pick up his cycle from where it leant against the wall of the house, another smile, her second that day, pulled at long-set muscles. She called after him: "George, you'll never guess! I was christened Beatrice, but I couldn't stand it – that's why the 'Trixie', and don't you ever tell a soul!"

He waved in reply as he went out of the gate. Her obvious delight had kindled his enthusiasm for the project. Anything to do with horses was, for George, a pleasure rather than work, and to set that young girl up with a pony and trap would be a great satisfaction for him, too. He went down the road to his home grinning widely, pleased he had thought of it. Trixie went indoors feeling hungry now and glad she could heat up the casserole George had brought. For the first time since Walter had gone, she began to look forward to something – in fact, she found she had already started to imagine what this pony would look like. At least, she reasoned, she would be able to afford to keep it. She was doing very well on her own so far and had no family except her animals to keep. A pony and trap would be a necessity for her to get about and, her mind made up, went to pick some vegetables to go with the stew.

The coal shifted in the grate of the black range and brought Trixie back to the present. She sat up straighter in her chair by the fire and looked down at Inky, still a handsome cat in his blue-black coat and good in the house, too, not like some tomcats who sprayed indoors. This was pure luck. No one around thought to neuter their cats; apart from the unwanted expense it was thought that they must hold their own with the rest of the cat population. It was a sad fact that the many resulting kittens might well end up drowned if homes were not quickly found for them.

"You leave that poor old Sue alone, you wicked old cat," she warned him. Inky half-closed his eyes as he gazed back at Trixie. She'd watched him being chased and spat at this morning when he'd ventured near the mouser's quarters and he had run swearing from the onslaught. She'd put down some milk for Sue with a saucer of scraps. "Curiosity will be the death of you, if Sue doesn't get you first," she told him.

'Sitting around wouldn't butter any parsnips,' she thought. She had to stir herself away from the fire again before the afternoon ran away to early darkness. She got up and went to put on her outdoor boots and coat and rounding the corner of the house, was just in time to see Elsie's two boys pressing towards the windows of the evening school bus to give her a grin and a wave. It always cheered her and she waved back, watching the bus slowly and steadily wend its way down the lane, dropping off the children outside their home gates.

Chapter 13

Friday evening at just past three o'clock and the November day was already on the wane. The primary school children, chattering quietly under the watchful eye of a stern headmaster, formed lines inside the iron railings of the little school to wait for the bus that would take them home.

William looked for Barry, who was exchanging surreptitious blows with Alex, while holding his slipper bag at the string and thumping the heavy plimsolls within it across Alex's side. Alex dropped his bag to charge at Barry. "Watch out – headmaster," hissed William, lunging for Alex and catching him by the arm as he came past. Instantly, Alex ran back for his bag and he and Barry hurried to stand in line, both breathing hard and trying not to giggle. But in truth, all of the pupils from the four year-olds up to eleven, feared the wrath of Mr Thompson. He wore a long black jacket over pinstripes which emphasised his dark, brooding expression. He carried his head forward, and hunched, hands linked behind his back as he glowered fit to quell the most determined riot, never mind the light-hearted shenanigans of a few young boys. It was hard enough for the oldest class of children to learn from such a martinet and it was a mercy that the Misses taught the children in class.

Miss Carter taught the newest intake, the little four year olds. She was comfortingly mild when contending with the intermittent puddles from some of the more nervous children, and what a struggle it was for them to reach the lavatories in time. They were sited in separate rows on each side of the playground. Just wooden seats over buckets, no different for most of the children from those at their homes where they had to take a torch to the outhouse after dark, or even light a candle while they sat – the first experience of a candlelit occasion that they ever knew!

The school caretaker, who started his day lighting the big fires in the school rooms before the pupils arrived for lessons, finished by carting all the buckets to a vast pit in the corner of the farm field adjoining the playground. The caretaker had to be a dedicated man.

Before the bus arrived, the pig man stopped outside the school gate, six great yawning bins jammed in the back of his small, flatbed lorry. Barry watched, fascinated as the man trundled the bins from the canteen. Beetroot juice – lots of it – spilled down the sides with other interesting leftovers to make a very curious mixture. He hated beetroot and shuddered at the sight of the oozing bins. Salad, today, had been followed by a cauldron of semolina manhandled from the small, steaming canteen by an army of stout, perspiring ladies to be ladled out on a trestle table set up in the classroom. He'd hoped he wouldn't get a lump of the stuff! After that, one of the dinners he most disliked, eaten because he felt too hungry to refuse (and he had the headmaster's eye on him) he had gone to the cold cloakroom to wash his hands. Becky Porter had picked up a small piece of the strong-smelling soap beside him and without preamble said, "Anyway, there's no Father Christmas." Barry stared at her, amazed. He carried on washing. Too big a stain on the roller towel was always noticeable. "There's no such thing as Father Christmas," Becky said again.

"How do you know? There is," said Barry stoutly.

"My brother said it's Dad," was the reply.

Barry had to think about this while he pulled the roller down in the hope of eventually finding a dry spot, and reached to wipe his hands. "Well, I know there is, because Mum said and she never tells lies," said Barry with an air of triumph.

Miss Harrington, hearing a lively scuffle issuing from the cloakroom next to her classroom, flung open the door and surveyed the muddle of two five-year-olds clutching and

73

pulling at each other's clothes. She sided with neither child, but bundled them both off to their classrooms with a scolding for being late for their lesson. All in all, it had not been Barry's day.

The children were starting to get cold standing in their thin socks and Wellingtons by the time the bus arrived. Mr Thompson watched the orderly queue climbing on board and sent to the back the one or two boys who pushed or rushed to get on. Some of the younger children had to sit on the laps of the older ones which caused some jostling but they knew the driver wouldn't start the bus until they were seated and quiet, so settling to the journey home was never prolonged.

Barry flung himself off the bus as soon as he could, raced up the track beside the house and found his mother just about to cut him and William each a large slice of bread pudding. They were always hungry after school. "Mum, Becky Porter says there's no such thing as Father Christmas, but there is isn't there. I told her, but she won't believe it, so I fought her and Miss Harrington came out and told us off." He picked up his slice of pudding and ate large bits off it as if for comfort. Elsie looked over Barry's head and caught William's knowing eye. William, at nine years old, must have tumbled to the truth before this but, bless him, he'd kept it from his brother.

"It's a pity Becky doesn't believe in Father Christmas, Barry. But you hang up your stocking, don't you, and it's always been filled. When did you ever find it empty?" Barry started to relax at this and slow down a bit. "If Becky doesn't believe Father Christmas will come, there won't be much point in hanging up her stocking will there?" which side-tracked Barry, much to Elsie's relief. She had always felt that the children in this rural neighbourhood went for long periods without anything very special happening to brighten their lives and like every mother, was determined to hang on to any treats for them for as long as she possibly could.

Chapter 14

William and Barry were walking home from school one day when they were astonished to see a tall, fine-boned black horse tossing along the road with a straight-faced lady sitting side-saddle. A veil fell wispily from a neat, black half-topper, and extended just beyond her small, retroussé nose. Her severely tailored black habit was relieved only by a stark, white stock.

It was a vision to be stared at in wonder and both boys watched, riveted to the ground, swivelling round as she rode past with no more than a brief nod to them. The apparition didn't speak, but trotted the glossy black horse on with a slow, exaggerated pace until horse and rider were out of sight.

Unusually lost for words, they would have said they had seen something rare, special. The horses and ponies they came across in their everyday lives were George's Suffolks or the ponies they had seen from time to time pulling small trade carts. This was a different species!

"Who was that?" Barry asked William, curiously.

"Never seen her before," answered William. "I wonder how she gets off that horse with that long skirt. I bet she trips up."

"Where's her other leg gone? How can she keep still?"

William shrugged and looked about. The hedges either side of the unmarked road were bobbed short and bare across the narrow ditches. The fields were flat with a great roof-shaped mound of cut sugar beet to the edge of one, the others were deeply furrowed with dark earth waiting to be re-planted in the spring. Against the grey flat monotony of the November afternoon, a few gulls lifted, feathers ruffled by the cutting wind and settled again on the plough.

"Come on, hurry up Barry, let's get home. I'm getting cold," said William and started to run. Barry shrieked as he always did at the thought of being left behind to follow on his own, and William slowed down to grab his hand. He wished now he'd come home on the bus with the others, instead of spending his bus fare at the ice cream van.

Elsie had seen Lady Munnings ride by earlier that day and knew she lived down the hill in Dedham Valley with Sir Alfred, the artist famous for his horse paintings, but when the boys told her about the black lady on the tall black horse, she looked surprised and impressed – she didn't want to steal their thunder. She could not understand why she should dress up like that just to ride out round the roads along here and fancied that she had just been sitting for Sir Alfred while he painted her and, like a child just let out of school, decided to set off for a ride while she was in the saddle and ready now to let rip – she couldn't wait to change!

Tom had also seen her come along the road from the little red brick railway bridge and when the skittish horse sidestepped as he neared the tractor, Tom switched off the engine and earned a grudging wave from the straight, slight-waisted figure.

"Come to see how the other half live," he grumbled to himself, but relished the sight even so. It was a treat to see a beautiful horse ridden well with such style – something which was for him quite out of the ordinary. There was no time, money or teacher for people he knew to aspire to such an accomplishment, should the possibility ever cross their minds.

His attention was caught by smoke rising, seemingly out of the field in front of him. The column chased along to the railway bridge where it rose in a whoosh either side as the train cluttered underneath it and rattled on with a business-like rhythm. "That would have set her Ladyship back a bit if she was crossing the bridge with that rare horse just then," he mused with a grin. "Don't know what I'd have done if she'd

76

landed on her bustle and the horse had gone off across the field."

Sighing, he leaned forward to start the tractor up once more and turned it for the next row.

Although Elsie was used to the boys sometimes walking the two miles home from school, she had just started to get anxious as they walked in. There weren't so many families in their community that each didn't know the others or their children and it engendered a feeling of safety for them. So long as Elsie and Alan were told where they were off to, the children were usually free to come and go but the evenings were cold and dark now, and she didn't want them to walk home any more at this time of year.

That morning Elsie had made her Christmas cake and while it was baking had walked up the road to visit Gwen Williams. Gwen and Toby had moved here with their daughter from Wales several years ago at a time when there were more than a few cases of TB around the coal mining areas there. Toby had wanted to get away from the pits and start afresh working above ground. Now had come the appalling discovery of their only daughter's illness. Gwyneth had TB and at the age of seventeen, when she should have been enjoying freedom and youth, and was confined to a bed in the living room. Gwen and Toby had struggled with the authorities to be allowed to keep her at home but the day-to-day strain of looking after her sometimes resulted in quarrels between the two and Gwyneth would scare them by getting unsteadily to her feet to try to intervene. Gwen was almost as housebound as Gwyneth when Toby was working while she gave her daughter every care.

"He's so awful sometimes," Gwen told Elsie in the kitchen, so as not to disturb Gwyneth, asleep now. "Here we are trying to pull together, and now Toby says she should be in a sanatorium! We agreed from the start that we would try to keep her here with us. It's what Gwyneth wanted. Now he says we can't cope."

"What does the doctor say?" asked Elsie, playing for

77

time. She really didn't know what was best for Gwyneth. How could the young girl bear being sent away for months or years to recover in a remote hospital, if she could be at home?

"He says if it becomes too much, we are to tell him and she must go away, just as if we are likely to do that! Most days we can get by, and we do so want her with us. If it helps Gwyneth to recover more quickly, of course we want her here, but Toby and I don't always get on and worry about Gwyneth is an added strain."

Elsie, looking glum, did not know how to comfort Gwen, who caught the expression on Elsie's face. Lifting her chin and smiling a little, Gwen said, "Thanks for slipping along to see us, love. It's such a treat to have your company. Let's take this tray through and see if Gwyneth's awake. I know she likes to see you and have you to talk to."

Gwen put some biscuits on a plate and picked up the tray with the tea she had been making and she and Elsie crept quietly into the living room where the heat from the fire hit them as they walked in. Gwyneth stirred and turning over, opened her eyes. "Just in time," said Gwen and poured some tea for her. Elsie thought Gwyneth looked beautiful with clear, pale skin, dark hair and large, hazel eyes. How much longer would she have to lie like this while her young life passed her by?

"I'm off on Saturday to Colchester to buy some Christmas stuff," Elsie said. "Is there anything I can bring back for either of you while I'm there?"

"Could you change my book, please?" asked Gwyneth, reaching for a library book lying on the bed. There was the county library in Colchester now as well as the one that had done them for years which was a private one making a small charge for borrowed books down North Hill – the only library until the county one opened.

Elsie took the book back with her as she walked home to take her cake out of the oven.

She paused as she straightened up with the cake wrapped a cloth. How on earth would she cope if one of her family became so ill? Polio cropped up from time to time too, and one of the children in William's class had to walk in callipers. The cake became hot in her hands and brought her back from her dark thoughts. "Carry on and don't think about every mother's nightmare," she told herself.

Chapter 15

Saturday morning, pocket money day, and 6d richer, William and Barry went across the road to Betty and Brian's home to see if they'd be walking up to Mrs Brown's that morning. Sweet rationing was still in force, but it really wasn't a problem for the children. 6d just didn't go very far. The walk to the shop, however, was beset with distractions for them all, and could take the best part of a morning.

They crossed the empty road and cut into a square field wet with long grass. The two smaller children, Barry and Brian, struggled to keep up in their hampering Wellingtons which tangled with the folded grass. William and Betty were running towards the wire fence which bordered the deep cut to the railway line below. All of them heard the train long before they saw the smoke hit the small red brick bridge and divide and emerge from the short tunnel to billow in clouds either side.

"We should have been quicker," puffed William, "We could have stood on the bridge while it went under." They all walked past the disused sandpit and down to the wood, listening for the next train. A whole group of children had been round the walnut tree in October but the walnuts they had eaten then were now forgotten, the tree as bare as most of the mixed trees in the wood. The tallest trees still bore the crossed twigs of the rookery, quiet now till the next season. The leaves underfoot were sodden and a dirty, uniform brown, but the laurels were still green, though their shiny broad leaves were dulled from the sooty train smoke. Brian's hands were already black from touching a few as he walked past.

Out the other side of the wood, and they were fascinated

to discover that the field usually dotted with placid cows had been part fenced for a flock of some hundred turkeys, all black, the females piping in high complaint answered by the heavy, stiff-strutting males in painful-sounding gobbles. Standing across the road to watch the turkeys at a distance was not good enough, and Barry found a stick to run along the chicken-wire fence to see what happened. The nearest cock turkey lost no time – he ran at the fence and gobbled his anger straight at Barry who, standing there shocked, and still, didn't look much taller than the great bird. Deciding to leave well alone, the children backed away and continued along the road.

"I wonder who's going to kill and pluck all those turkeys?" Betty asked.

"I expect they'll all end up in the packing shed," answered William, impressed at the thought.

Betty pointed at a large, still beetle in front of her. "Looks a bit dead to me," said Brian. "I'll dead it a bit more," said Barry and went to jump on it. William got fed up waiting for Barry sometimes – he felt held back when he really wanted to move through life a lot faster. Barry plonked down suddenly in the road to take a stone out of his boot. "Oh, come on, Barry, the shop will be shut by the time we get there!" Mrs Brown closed for her elevenses. There was just Billy to call as they went past his field before they would reach journey's end at the shop, and the little brown pony came trotting up pleased for the children's company and accepted the bruised strips of wet grass that Betty offered across the gate. "He's lonely in there on his own," she said.

Mrs Brown was also on her own today and glad of a diversion when the four children trooped in. She was used to helping them choose their sweets and, of course they took a long time. Black jacks or gob-stoppers. Toffee shards, liquorice allsorts, dolly mixtures – the litany had to be gone through. Barry always wanted chewing gum.

"You know your Mum won't let you have it, Barry. How is your Mum, anyway?" to distract him.

Barry thought and dimly remembered a phrase he'd heard over at Brian's one afternoon, when the visitor had looked very impressed and had raised her eyebrows in surprise. "She's no better than she ought to be," he said clearly, and was gratified to see Mrs Brown raise her eyebrows too. He bet she thought that a very grown-up thing to say.

Home later, the sweets just a happy memory, Elsie met them with "There you are! I wondered what had happened to you both, you've been gone so long. What have you been up to?"

"The train just missed us," said William, "and a turkey attacked Barry, but he had a stick to fight back, so that was all right. Brian didn't like his nut toffee so he gave it to Billy on the way home. He enjoyed it – I think. He took a long time to chew it. When's dinner, Mum, I'm hungry!"

The children had woods, fields, footpaths and hedgerows to explore and often they went off on warm days for a picnic, taking sandwiches and bottles of squash to a field they knew where there was a small, clear stream which washed through some watercress beds. The stream discharged into a pool which they set to dam one golden afternoon, stripped to their underwear, up to their ankles in clear-running water while the sweltering passengers in passing steam trains waved forlornly out of smutty windows and longed to be young again.

One day George the farm hand along the lane to the shop lost the red and white Hereford bull on the way to the field. The rope which attached the ring to the chain he was holding broke and the bull ran freely across the road and along a track beside the railway crossing just as William and Barry with Betty and Brian were on their way to the shop.

"You kids get back in the wood," he shouted and shot after the bull. They stood and watched transfixed as he raced after it. The cows, who had been steadily walking ahead of George and the bull, now scattered in the turmoil and went in all directions. George turned as he ran and saw the children still standing, mesmerised. He raced back to the witless children, scooped them up together safely and led them back into the wood. He opened the field gate and the cows, glad to see a place they recognised, flowed through into the meadow. George was left to intercept the bull who turned to follow. George shut the gate after the bull had ambled through, then leaned over it with his head in his hands. He looked as if he was praying.

For the children, this was unlooked-for entertainment, and enlivened their walk to the shop that day. The trip there was always as much a dawdle as coming back, while they ate the sweets they had taken so long to choose.

Chapter 16

Alex was awake at 7 a.m. on Sunday morning and he turned his head on the pillow to look at Rosie asleep on her tummy in the cot, her fine fair hair curling across a cheek as pink as a gentle dawn. His mother was already downstairs and he could hear her vigorously poking the embers in the range to renew the fire whilst the kettle was boiling. He stretched and snuggled under the warm cover. Mum and Dad took turns at these chores at the weekend and maybe, if he was quiet, he could steal into their bed and have a good cuddle before Rosie woke and demanded all their attention.

Downstairs, Peggy opened the door to the cat who dropped a live mouse at her feet. It immediately sought sanctuary under the sideboard while the cat stalked, concentrated and with measured steps, after it.

"Oh, you wicked little devil! Jack, your cat's got a mouse again," Peggy called up the stairs. "I don't know where he keeps finding them." The cat was always Jack's when he'd caught a mouse.

"No rest for the wicked, Alex," muttered Jack as he sprinted out of the bed and tucked his pyjama legs into his big, thick socks. No telling where a terrified mouse might run. Alex was a step behind – it was usually worth watching his parents capering round the room each time this happened – and sat with the stair door open, two steps up out of the way. Peggy curled her legs up on a chair, sitting sideways, while Jack shooed the cat away. He made a dive under the sideboard to chase the mouse out of the open door. Rosie woke up and bawled for attention and the kettle whistled 'steam up' on the hob. Sunday morning in the Whitley household was underway.

Alex always protested at having to attend afternoon Sunday school but he had to go anyway. William and Barry called for him today and they all went to the big hut together.

All three were fortunate that they didn't have morning chores at the weekend like some of the children on the smallholdings.

There were one or two large families where a dozen or more of the children were still at home. Each child had an allotted task from feeding the chickens and pigs to peeling the vegetables for all their meals. The older girls had to help with the younger children and with whatever housework could be achieved in such crowded conditions in homes with no bathroom. This left the poor, overworked mothers to cope with a daily grind of trying to keep everything ticking over and everyone fed. At night, the boys and girls in separate bedrooms slept head to toe as best they could, and hoped the oldest would be married and out of the bed before the next youngster would put into the bed on the opposite side!

Annie Morgan, who lived next door to Bella, was the 'Reverend's' stalwart helper. Each Sunday, she stood in her black hat at the door of the huge hut which was set on steddles, making a preliminary count of heads as they rounded the corner of the packing shed on their way to Sunday school. No one was quite sure of the Reverend's qualifications for the job of teaching religion to these small sinners but these same small sinners were in no doubt as to Annie Morgan's powers to persuade them along the straight and narrow. As soon as the three boys spotted Annie in scouting mode, they made directly for the gaps between the steddles and hid under the hut.

Peggy, coming along later, walked up to the door holding Rosie on reins. Rosie had sat down so many times, enraged at being fettered that Peggy had had to resort to half-dragging her along on her bottom while she screamed blue murder – such was the general enthusiasm of Annie's little flock for the coming lessons.

At the final muster for the first hymn, Benny the post,

being drawn this week to play the piano while the regular pianist was away, asked, "And what's the text for today, Mrs M?" She stood looking round, perplexed. "Suffer the little children to come unto me," she replied promptly, "but I can't find the little sods anywhere!" She and the Reverend heard the titters and, bending down to see under the hut, caught the grinning children huddled underneath. With the remaining young congregation hollered into order, the piano set the notes for the first hymn.

The next Sunday school treat would be the Christmas Party and there was therefore very good attendance from the children each week to acquire the necessary coloured stamps for their stamp books to qualify for a special present from Father Christmas. At the end of the session, under the watchful eye of Peggy behind them, still wrestling with Rosie, the three boys queued up for their highly coloured stamps depicting that holy week. Then, in accordance with the Reverend's fervent advice that they lift up their hearts unto the Lord, they did just that as they raced for home and freedom.

The other Sunday school treat, eagerly looked forward to by the children, was a trip to the seaside. Most of the mothers groaned when the day came for this one. Come rain or shine, the venue never changed. Although all hoped for at least a warm day, very often it was wet and cold and had to be undertaken with something of the well-remembered Dunkirk spirit. Annie always wore the black hat. It was for weddings and funerals too. She rallied the children on the beach to her banner stuck resolutely into the best spot above high-tide, her hat always recognised from a distance.

It seemed the job of taking the children on this Trip always fell to the mothers, the fathers having gardening or something else virtuous to do on that particular Sunday. At best it was a sunny, social occasion for the women, at worst a cold huddle on the beach while they tried to find enough pocket money for the children to spend on the pier. Next, they had to pull the girls out of clingy, wet stretchy-elastic swimming costumes and scoop them up in a towel to rub red and dry. Then they had to persuade the boys to come in despite their hardy determination to swim however cold, they so seldom had the chance to do so.

From time to time there was the Caravan Mission to Village Children. A missionary was sent round to the Sunday schools in rural areas to tell the children how the Church were converting the heathens to Christianity and how much it would cost to carry on bringing these black children the Word to turn them from their own beliefs to the true one.

On those Sundays the children were asked to give a little more for the collection, but some parents were heard to mutter that these missionaries should mind their own bloody business, let the black people worship their own gods and stop interfering. It wouldn't make the natives any happier, would it?

There was always a good attendance from the tenants at the Harvest Festival, for most one of the main events in the religious year. The hymns were well-known favourites, expected and sung with gusto. All the children took fruit, flowers and vegetables which were used to decorate the hut. This produce was later sent to the hospital in Colchester. All the youngsters who could be inveigled into it learned poems and songs to give a small concert for the parents at the service.

These activities seemed to suffice for the majority of the tenants on the Settlement, though most enjoyed a robust Carol singing at Christmas. Some of the men worked up quite a thirst along with the bonhomie engendered by a good old Carol singing, which took them straight to the pub afterwards.

There was a church in the village, one at each end of the Settlement. For weddings and funerals, Christenings and such, it was possible to take your pick. The church at Ardleigh, where Bella and Tom were married all those years ago, was in the centre of the village where there were two grocers, a hairdresser, a blacksmith and a fish and chip shop.

A fish and chip dinner was considered by all to be a special treat. It was as near, in those days, to eating out as most experienced.

The church at the opposite end of the Settlement, at Lawford, stood high on a hill with a magnificent view of the River Stour. This church had a grand setting but there was only one shop in the village, a general store no bigger than the Settlement's small local one. The only other significant building at this end was the village school attended by all the Settlement children until they were eleven years old. The school bell was feeble compared with the pealing of the five church bells ringing from the hilltop. Tom said a view was all very well but heaven knew those in the graveyard didn't need it and by the time the congregation had toiled their way up the hill to the church, they were too puffed out to gasp out a hymn, let alone have the strength to walk round the churchyard admiring the view. He was also put out by the 'high church' service. "All that chanting and carrying on," he said testily.

"You haven't much of a singing voice," Bella commented to him. "That's why you're not too keen." In fact, he was tone deaf, but Bella thought the setting of the church perfect for the sound of the organ as it winged across the Stour valley. It reminded her of a time when she was a girl and had cycled to East Bergholt across the river at Flatford.

There, one bright blowy morning, she had pushed her bicycle up the hill beside the wall of the monastery where the Franciscan friars were chanting the day's responses. She had found a seat half-way up the hill and sat watching pink chestnut candles tossing in the wind and listened for a while, enjoying the richness of the singing. It sent her cheerfully on her way, reassured that there would be many more unexpected, happy interludes like this to come in her life.

It was not something that she felt she could have easily shared with Tom, who liked the cheeriness of Sandy Macpherson at the theatre organ of a weekday morning when he was at home, the sound of which she secretly detested.

Happy and involved as she'd always been with Tom and her day-to-day busy life, there were times when she looked beyond their narrow confines and wondered about the future of her grandchildren and the lives they would lead. She and Tom had never travelled farther than London or the coast and although they had read about and seen films of foreign countries, they were unlikely ever to venture abroad. The only travellers they knew were those who had been abroad to fight in the last war – and they didn't recommend it.

Count your blessings; be content with what you have. They had all been thankful to live with these maxims while the country was still reeling from the war, getting on their feet again while contending with basic living and a gradual emergence from rationing. They would not and should not keep the youngsters from striving for better and broader lives. She wondered how this would all come about. Nothing, she found, was handed on a plate and any ambitions or aspirations would have to be gained against all odds, so far as she could see. There appeared to be just three avenues that the girls could reasonably take: shop assistant, nurse, or to carry on at the Technical College in a course in commerce to learn shorthand and typing. Very few parents living on the Settlement could afford to allow their children an extra year while keeping them at school or college. Most, stretched as they were, saw them into their first job with relief.

Education favoured the boys right from the start, when there were just three eleven-plus Grammar School places for the boys and two for the girls available to go from the local primary school. It was generally assumed, anyway, that the girls would leave work when they married to bring up children. The boys were given more attention in choosing their careers, and some chose the forces, carrying on after their National Service as a way to get out of farming. Others took a bus into town each day to learn printing or mechanics when they immediately earned more than the girls.

Bella wondered how much of their potential would her grandchildren be able to realise with their basic, limited education and opportunities. Elsie had learned shorthand and typing at evening classes and so was confident enough to take the part-time job at the solicitors, which seemed to suit her lively outlook on life and use her abundant young energy. Jack had studied accountancy on a commercial course which had benefited him more than they could have thought possible. He now had an important job keeping the accounts at the packing shed, but she knew they were the exception rather than the rule and, of course, a lot of the children were quite content to carry on doing what they'd been doing before school – imbibing the ways of running a smallholding or small farm.

"A crystal ball is what you need, my girl," she said, giving herself a mental shake. She rarely had time in her busy days to stop and think like this. Mooning about would get her nowhere.

There was always some job that needed doing and she pulled her old Singer sewing machine from the cupboard beside the fire. She fetched two plain white sheets and tore each in half down the middle where the fabric had worn thin and, turning the sides inwards, began stitching the first sheet down in a French seam. When they were seamed down the middle, she turned each side under. They would do for another length of time on the bed and save her having to buy new ones, since they were still very white from the weekly boil in the copper. Turning sheets sides to middle was not work which needed much concentration, but having something physical to do usually jogged Bella out of an introspective mood.

Chapter 17

When Jack called in to pick the children up, Bella was getting the ingredients for her Christmas pudding together on the big square table in the kitchen. She and Tom had been looking after Alex and Rosie on Saturday while Jack and Peggy had an evening at the Odeon in Colchester.

He found Rosie standing on a kitchen chair at the sink blissfully 'washing up', the floor awash and her front soaking. She gave a big grin when she saw her father and tried to scramble off the chair. He caught the two-year-old in mid-jump. There was no need to ask her if she'd had a good time with her Granny. It was a good job she always had a change of clothes here – she always seemed to get into a mess when she stayed overnight. "Wet," she said happily as Jack wafted her away at arm's length to find dry clothing.

Alex, at five years, had been promised a stir of the Christmas pudding mixture – three times round and make a wish and it will come true if you have your eyes shut, Granny had told him. Jack had always thought this a dangerous promise. Alex was now with Tom (following him around on his day off) out in the garden picking runner beans. Tom watched the concentration on Alex's face as he carefully picked each bean and put it in the chip basket they shared. Alex was remembering when he'd last seen the Jones's television one Sunday evening, sitting on the floor with all the other five and six year-olds, enthralled, watching the junior programme.

"How do televisions work, Grandad?" he asked. Tom was unprepared for this and suddenly realised he hadn't a clue. He'd understood that a wireless worked by soundwaves, he'd been told, but how pictures got onto a remote screen, he'd never found out.

"Have you asked your teacher?" he hedged. Miss Carter should know, I expect, if you ask her." Alex was almost sure his Grandad didn't know the answer. Well, he hadn't got a television either of course, but he had heard his Mum talking to Dad about getting one soon for when the Queen was crowned. He might be able to see a queen crowned. Pictures on a television!

"When will a queen be crowned, Grandad?" was the next question. Tom was up to this one. "In June – the next June that comes along, Alex," he said. "That's after Christmas, after the daffodils come, and after you have your Easter eggs. A long time to wait. Why?"

"I think Mum and Dad were talking about us having a television," he said. "Why is everything such a long time to wait. Why isn't anything today?" he added with impatience.

Bella loved having all the Grandchildren to stay. She was very proud of her son Jack – he was the chief accountant at Foxash and had an office off the packing shed. He earned enough now to run a car, a little black Austin which he'd bought second-hand. She thought it looked rather like a top hat, but it was his pride and joy, and he was one of the few people on the Settlement to have a car other than the motors used for work. There was the aptly named 'Jones' family across the road and up a few doors from Jean's home, who seemed to have the latest everything and caused more than a little envy among a few neighbours. They had a Ford Prefect car for, it seemed, mostly Sunday afternoon rides. To the amusement of many of the other wives, Henry would bring the car to the top of the steps sloping up from their house and stand by the door ready to open it when Mrs Jones tottered to the side in very high-heeled sandals, her blonde hair done just-so. Having ensconced his lady wife and shut the door very gently, he then ran swiftly round the back of the little green car and took his place in the driving seat. One of the women had been heard to mutter that "She didn't look much like that when she was packing the tomatoes in the shed all last week."

However, when their television was delivered, the Joneses invited many of the young children, including Alex, round on a Sunday evening to watch their favourite programmes, which won all the neighbours round.

Jack brought Rosie back into the kitchen and set her down on a chair next to Bella. He looked thoughtful and wondered whether to mention to his mother the gossip he had overheard in the packing shed when his door was open one day last week. Plump Jane, with a saucy look had nudged Dora and said she'd heard the baker's wife was spending a lot of time with that old Jim Macaulay, and gave one of her loud shouts of laughter. Dora intrigued, said "Well, they are sort-of next-door-neighbours."

"Yes, but she weren't delivering bread when my friend saw them," replied Jane, her round face merry.

That was when Jack, distracted by hearing the rumour, got up and shut the door. He hoped it wasn't true. The women there were always livening up their day with tit-bits like that, true or not. He'd known Sally since he'd grown up with her and her brother. They'd played together from when they were very young children. He saw when she became smitten with Peter at 16 how she had eyes only for him from that time. He'd always thought Peter very spoilt by his parents who doted on him and gave him whatever he wanted, so long as they could afford it. Jack was four years older than those two, and lost touch a little when he left school and went to work.

"Have you seen Jean lately, Mum?" he asked eventually,

Bella put a few sultanas into an eggcup and passed them to Rosie who said "Ohh," as if she'd been given a fortune. She took them out slowly, one at a time, and rolled them between her fingers, enjoying the squishy feel.

"She's not been over this week, but I expect she'll wait 'til she's done the curtains now." Bella looked unconcerned as she started weighing the dried fruit ready to pick out any little stones or stalks before putting it in the colander to wash under the running tap. So she's not heard anything, thought Jack relieved, and resolved not to say any more on the subject.

Bella turned from the sink just in time to stop Rosie from tipping the sticky sultanas into the sieved flour. She could do without help like that!

Chapter 18

It was a bitter Monday morning for the children to start the next week at school. Grannie Cafferty's granddaughter, Betty, who lived two doors along from Bella had been cycling there and back since she was seven years old. At that time, Miss Harrington, her schoolteacher, had agreed with Betty's mother that she would keep an eye on Betty while they both cycled the three miles along the road, just until Betty got used to the journey, when she would go on her own. Betty used to wait for Miss Harrington until she saw her coast over the railway bridge on her tall bicycle, her books in a huge wicker basket in front and a cover over the mudguard of her back wheel to keep her long skirts from catching.

Lately, Betty had been arriving at school, her legs blue and chapped in her school skirt, and was now plagued with the irritation of chilblains, like most of the children at this time of year.

At school, the teachers allowed the pupils to keep their coats on, the fires glowed as hot as was possible and the small bottles of frozen milk were lined up by the stove rails to thaw which, for some of the children, would be the first food they would have that day. The main school room was huge, the ceilings high, and this room housed two classes, separated by a large blackboard. Betty, within her class of nine year olds, did her best to concentrate on the lessons, endeavouring to write neatly with pen and ink while her hands were stiff with cold. Each class did its best to block out the occasional loud noises from the other, while they worked on their different subjects.

The one-room building was supplemented at this school by two large wooden huts. In one of these, the other spinster teacher, Miss Carter, held her class. If there was any compensation for the four and five year olds, abruptly leaving the security of their homes for the first time to be thrust into a classroom full of strange children, it was in the shape of Miss Carter who, having lost her sweetheart in the war, devoted her life to her 'babies'. She would scoop up and hug an unhappy child on its first foray into the outside world and sit them in a chair next to her. She would sit at her big desk raised on a dais reading her class a story with, more often than not, a small child sitting on her lap whom she mopped up from time to time with a large piece of white sheeting torn off from who knows where. If a new four year old looked like falling asleep, the teacher would put two tables together and make a bed with coats to let them rest, rather than try to teach the alphabet to such a sleepy-head. For a child who had to get used to school in this suddenly changed world, she was their salvation. There were no nursery schools to break them in gently.

There she sat at her desk, where her round glasses enabled her to survey her little captives in friendly beam. She was usually dressed in a square, green tweed suit, unless it was particularly warm, when she would take off her jacket to sit in her cool, neatly pressed, white blouse. Green, she felt, was the best colour to complement her short, very thick copper-coloured hair that stuck out from her head in a wedge of wiry frizz.

The older children went on to be given a good grounding in English and arithmetic, learning tables by rote and, since it was a strong Church of England school, the catechism was also learnt by heart, and all these subjects were checked from time to time by a visiting minister. Then, since theirs was such a rural life, there were lessons in crop rotation, flora and fauna, and even tables which measured rods, poles and perches, all of which equalled five and half yards antiquated as they already were in most schools.

Once a year in spring, the older children were led along the bank of a stream thick with frog and toad spawn, which started in the school field. They followed its progress to where it joined the estuary of the River Stour. The fascination of their tiny stream becoming part of this mighty river may not have been immediately appreciated by a class of small, weary children, but the distance they had just walked and their aching legs were certainly apparent to every child who took part.

Now, spring seemed far away and Betty was glad to be at an afternoon sewing lesson, sitting in Miss Harrington's classroom where the huge fire had finally made an impact on the whole room and the pupils could at last get warm before the cold homeward trek.

———————————

On the last day of term, the children trailed home from school carrying squashed, sticky paper chains, Alex's stuck flatly together half-way along for variation, but all admired by the adults. Peggy had called in to ask Bella if she'd like a lift into Colchester to buy the Christmas presents and goodies for which all the women had saved coupons and fruit-picking wages. Peggy couldn't drive, but Jack said he'd take them both on Saturday when her next-door neighbour could look after the children.

"I'll make a list tonight," said Bella, pleased.

Tom strode in the door with Alex following hot on his heels, "Blasted earwigs!" he said, as he kept to his straight course through the house. Bella lifted her eyes to the ceiling and glanced at Peggy with a 'tut'.

"Tom, the children will soon pick that up, swearing like that," she said.

"Eary, eary, eary-wig," said Rosie with satisfaction.

"Well, at least she picked the right word up," said Peggy.

Tom turned from washing his earth-caked hands in the sink, Alex following suit, always happy to closely follow his Grandfather.

"It's woodlice that have had those onions under the shed

97

roof, Tom," she said. "Anyway, there's more to life than onions! Peggy and I are off to town on Saturday to buy some things for Christmas. Elsie says you can go to hers for dinner if you'd like, or maybe you fancy a little time on your own."

"I'll finish that bit of digging, then slip up to Elsie's midday," said Tom, pulling down his shirt sleeves. Bella hoped he'd leave her flower patch alone, now set with spring bulbs. She was amazed at Tom sometimes. Ploughing wide stretches of land as he did on the tractor, he continued to use a broad brush when it came to the more intricate planting in the garden. He nearly always had to ask her what to plant and when, and never seemed to know the names of her flowers. Tom was forbidden to weed in her patch, while she took charge of the flowers and kept a sharp eye on him when he was gardening. She'd lost too many good plants that way.

Now she and Peggy squashed in the back of the little black Austin on a Saturday teeming with rain. Bella strained to see over Jack's shoulder through the steamed up window while the wipers did their best to clear the windscreen. Jack was going to go straight back home to pick up the children. The two women were glad to have the freedom to get cracking on their own and instead of a leisurely treat, felt a concentrated scoot round to gather what they could in this weather might be the order of the day. They separated and arranged to meet at the bus park for the home journey. Bella was walking past the WI shop where she bought her fertile hens' eggs in spring with her black umbrella pulled over her eyes batting into the wind and rain, her bag hanging heavy with the morning's shopping, when two happy voices coming the other way caused her to raise her umbrella sharply to be confronted with Sally turning to laugh at Jim Macaulay who walked along with his two arms holding Sally close, wrapping her up against the wet, and smiling back at her. Bella tried to sidestep with an apology, but it was too late.

"Hello Bella," muttered Sally, her head down now and shy. Jim Macaulay nodded and manoeuvred on the pavement to walk past Bella and take Sally on and away. Bella felt her colour rise and was confused and tongue-tied. She had known Sally since a baby but it was none of her business. She wanted to shake her! She had never really liked Peter. It was none of her business! She nodded and gave both of them a grave "Hello", and walked sadly on, wanting to get away and think it out. Did Jean know, she wondered?

Chapter 19

Earlier that morning and right at the other end of the Settlement at the bakery on the outskirts of Ardleigh, Peter was setting out small plots of dough to bake rolls.

"I'll be off then," said Sally sweeping into the big, hot room. He now employed a fourteen-year-old on Saturday mornings in an effort to please Sally, but Simon seemed slow and unco-ordinated, his limbs conspiring to trip him up if he attempted to work faster. Peter missed quick and capable Sally who had been his 'right hand' girl all these years. He hoped Simon would soon pick up the idea of taking the used equipment to the sink and washing it up without always being told - that would be such a help – still, it was only Simon's second Saturday at the bakery. Patience. Peter had had plenty of practice lately to exercise *patience.*

Peter was still confused at what had happened between him and Sally. There they were, not so long ago working side by side and doing a demanding job. Now – all of a sudden, it seemed – it wasn't good enough for her; she wanted more, or even a different life. Women were never satisfied. He'd heard that before, but it seemed waiting for her to 'come to her senses' was a waste of time. He knew no other life, had been brought up to carry on with the bakery – she knew that well enough at the start.

Last week they had had another confrontation. She had announced, "I think I'd better move into the spare bedroom for the time being, Peter. I'm not sleeping at all well lately and I know I disturb you and it's hard for me to keep still and quiet."

"How long is that going to go on?" he had asked. Things were getting bad and he didn't know how to stop it. "Look, I don't mind if you can't sleep, it hardly wakes me." Then, "Look, dammit, you've no right to go off like that – you're my wife!" Everything he said seemed to make the situation worse.

"You know you can't cope so well with the day's work if you're up half the night when I keep you awake. Anyway, all you really care about is your business and making money, Peter, so don't you try to persuade me back in with you."

He was astounded. How had things got this far? Why didn't he just say he loved her, wanted her to be happy, but he felt she had made plain her feelings of rejection of him. He would not risk his pride. Instead he said, "I'll get some help in on Saturday mornings to do a bit of the routine work – how does that sound?"

He thought she looked a lot more cheerful after that and felt he'd done the best he could for now. When she closed the spare room door on him that night she gave him a small smile and said it would only be for the time being, until she got back into the sleep routine again.

Today he stood gazing at her dumbly. She had on her good grey coat, belted to show her slim waist, her hair shining and tidy, its weight caught at the back in the way he loved. There was a glow about her which he knew had nothing to do with the hot room in which she was standing. He supposed it went with her high determination to be a little more independent and a little to do with the excitement of a day's Christmas shopping in town with the money she'd saved.

The rain was bouncing off the road outside and rushing down the windows.

Although it was so wet, she was wearing her good patent black shoes she set such store by.

"Do you have your brolly with you?" he asked, concerned.

She picked it up from beside her as she walked over to look out of the window at the beating rain. "I'll wait until I see the bus coming along and then run for it," she said, "I'll

101

wait in the porch."

Then, miserably, Peter watched her board the bus.

Jim Macaulay parked his van just off the bus park, turned up the collar of his rain mac and ran to Sally, just getting off the bus. She started towards him, then stopped and looked round. Neither of them must forget they lived in a small neighbourhood where everyone knew each other. How long would it be before someone spotted them together, and seeing them together, reached the right conclusion?

Chapter 20

That same Saturday morning, Alan rounded up William and Barry for their annual shopping trip to the town.

"Come on you two, let's get out from under your mother's feet and get a few presents with your pocket money. Then you can wrap them up yourselves."

"With our pocket money?" piped up Barry, as if it was the most unheard of thing. "I haven't got much!"

"You'll both have enough for what you'll need to buy, I'm sure, we'll 'cut our coat according to our cloth', though it will fit a bit tight!"

William glanced up at his father wryly. "I think I'll have to settle for a jacket," he said.

They walked from the bus station, hurrying along in the rain, straight to Woolworth's where William, sniffing 'Californian Poppy' perfume found it so 'disgusting' that he had to take the only alternative, a small blue, more intriguing bottle of 'Evening in Paris'. He was determined he would buy his mother perfume, which he thought an exotic present for her. Alan wondered if he and Elsie could live with the smell, but encouraged his elder son's choice all the same.

Barry settled for a huge, blue jar of bath salts which he thought looked a very big, impressive present for his Mum and wondered how he could spirit two pencils and a small ruler to the counter as well, and pay for them as a present for his Dad, without him seeing. William had sidled round the big square counter and found a few books on the next. 'Forever Amber' was a lively-looking paperback, bright, with an attractive lady illustrated on the cover. He slipped a copy away from his father's gaze to take to the till with the perfume. Dad always said he liked a good book.

Alan could see the boys looking 'hunted' and filtering quietly away, so he wandered off a little to give them room to manoeuvre. He knew William would help Barry to sort things out at the till. They liked to buy something to surprise him – was he in for a surprise!

Shopping in Colchester was always a big event for the boys. One of the treats of the day was to go to the fish and chip restaurant in a small side street and sit by the steamed-up front window putting all the vinegar, salt and pepper they thought they could get away with on the piping hot cod and chips. If the budget ran to an ice cream afterwards, while Alan enjoyed a strong cup of tea in a thick, white cup, then that was the height of bliss. This would have the two boys bouncing along the street chatting afterwards, warm and happy, off to catch the bus home.

There was always a sidling in the door as soon as they arrived home from a present-buying expedition. A quick 'hallo' to Elsie, then an exaggerated clatter upstairs to their bedroom to hide the presents. Loud, indignant words would come from Barry a moment later, when William selected the very same place Barry had that instant decided was the spot to hide his presents.

"How did it go, then?" Elsie asked Alan who had shaken his wet coat out of the door, and was now steaming himself dry in front of the range, while she put some bread and butter on a plate. She brought a pot of honey out of the cold, north-facing cupboard which held all their food (no refrigerators for anyone about there at that time) and put it on the table with some buns she had made that afternoon.

Alan put his arms round the back of her waist as she bent forward over the table and snuggled his head against her neck. "You know I enjoy that little excursion just before Christmas, it always puts me in the mood!"

Elsie slowly wound round in his arms and tried to look unmoved and distant, but it didn't suit her. She could never hold such a look at Alan for long. Instead, she took his face in her hands and gave him a big, hard, kiss, then, "Unhand me, sir, before things go to pieces, the perishers will be down in just a minute, and you know you can't resist me."

Alan laughed and let her go, swiping a bun from around her as he did. "Loving don't last and cooking do – but you make some lovely buns," he said and it was gone in two lusty bites.

Right now, one of the good things for Alan at home was a blessed holiday from heaving large trays of tomatoes and vegetables aboard a slow, heavy lorry and shifting reluctant gears to roll it up to London. There, the unloading was done, mostly by him, with minimal equipment to help it all off. Sometimes the sheer boredom of the job numbed his mind and he looked forward to and appreciated this time with Elsie and the boys.

He had spent many cold evenings in the shed making William a wooden battleship from rough packing-box wood he'd gleaned. He'd sanded down the hull and used plywood pieces to make the superstructure, all painted grey and green. He'd fitted a mousetrap mechanism in the hull which when triggered by a ball rolled against the wooden button on the side of the ship, blew the superstructure pieces into the air, all to be built up again. He had found the scooter for Barry easier to construct once he had traded his boat plans, such as they were, for two small wheels, but he was doubtful that he'd got the height of the handlebars right for Barry without measuring him up. He would simply have to adjust the size later. He had put some lonely hours into these projects and was rather proud of them. He just hoped the boys would be happy with their surprises.

They had almost got the stocking presents together and found that peace could be better achieved at Christmas if they put similar items in both stockings, which were two old nylon ones Elsie had saved. They started with the traditional orange, apple, and nuts. A big colouring book with crayons folded within might come next and a tin of Sharps toffees made up a bit more. The heavier the stocking became, the longer it stretched, and Alan and Elsie determinedly filled them right to the top with little toys. A chocolate Father Christmas always went in last to poke out of the top of the whole ensemble, and was the first thing each boy saw when he woke in the early hours. There was much tip-toeing, whispering and rustling from the parents as they carefully laid the stockings at the foot of each bed. There would be a few, magic, memorable days for the boys before the hastily stuck-together paper chains started drifting down and the holly stuck behind the pictures became hot and brittle and began to shift down the walls, littering dried red berries onto the floor.

Chapter 21

Sally, with so many bread orders to fulfil today, nevertheless stood idly at the table, deep in thought. She had managed to see Jim only once since their meeting in town. Again, she went over it.

She had gone in the van with Peter to stock up the larder. They had become so busy getting mince pies and Christmas cakes cooked, on top of their usual baking, that her own store cupboard had been neglected. Peter had gone to the barber's next door. She had walked into the shop while Jim stood at the counter. He shot her a fleeting look of question, and she quickly shook her head. He followed her glance back over her shoulder and with a nod walked by her and out of the shop. The shop bell clanged crossly as the door banged shut behind him. Sally could hardly believe that he had walked past her like that, close as they were, but there was no help for it. Rumours might well have started by now. Events seemed to be closing in on them.

She had insisted on continuing to use the spare bedroom despite Peter's questions and baffled looks. "It's no good, Peter, I can't sleep lately, anyway," and looking at her pale face, Peter could see that this was no lie. He watched her as she sat picking at the cuff of her cardigan with nervous tugs and said, "Look, Sally, just what is the matter, we can't carry on like this. You're always tired; you never smile any more. Frankly, you look ill – what's going on?"

She had looked up at him steadily for the first time in weeks and took in his drawn face. He seemed to have lost weight and looked smaller, less bluff and hearty than she'd known him (how long ago?) in one of his ebullient moods. He wasn't a bad husband, there were plenty worse. How do you tell a husband who believes he has given you everything, still wants to be with you and doesn't even know you are in love with another man – yet!

Miserably she'd lowered her eyes and picked up a bowl from the table to wash up. "I expect it'll all come right in the end," she'd muttered and turned to the sink to discourage his further questions.

She had been dreading he would find out from someone ever since she and Jim had bumped into Bella more than a week ago. She had kept away from her mother's home with the very good excuse that she and Peter were stretched with cake-making right up to Christmas. She had even got Peter to convey this message when he delivered the bread last week.

Now, with a sigh, she took one of the bowls of dough and slapped it upside down onto one of the boards on the large square table. She couldn't tell him yet, for if she did she would have to leave him flat just before Christmas with all the promised cakes to ice on top of all the extra cooking. For all his expertise in bread making, Peter couldn't ice Christmas cakes to save his life. Guilty and unhappy as she now felt, she couldn't compound her lack of loyalty by walking out on him just at this hectic time.

Jim was just as busy with the run-up to Christmas. Many of the men seemed to be using the few days before Christmas Day as a reason to call in for a quick drink with their workmates or whoever they met and Jim had his work cut out to reorder and stock up for the festive season.

No wonder she was in such a nervous state, she thought. Despite their lack of time right now she owed it to Peter to come out with it – if she dithered over how to put it for much longer, he would find out from neighbours or Jim would take a hand and she wanted to avoid that at all costs. With all the rushing around they had to do, she had hardly time to think straight right now, but this situation could not go on for much longer. She must be prepared, by the time the work subsided at Christmas, to tell Peter and get it over with.

After that, she and Jim could be free to go where they could start a new life – she must hold on to that!

Chapter 22

Bella knew by the way Tom came forcefully through the back door that he was 'in a tear' about something. "More than earwigs this time," she muttered as she calmly carried on ironing. 'Earwigs' was his blanket name for all garden pests which dared to eat his growing vegetables. When Tom came in complaining about blasted earwigs, Bella knew there was actually very little to worry about for the time being.

"I've heard it all now," he started. "What do you think? Poor old George – they've just told him – he's got to pack in looking after those two horses. Told him he's past it – good as. He's been biking up to those stables morning, noon and night. He knows they'll do away with them if he can't get up there. Poor old sod, in this cold weather he's nearly done in getting there as it is, then there's mucking out, carrying those water buckets, laying up the mangers – it's a wonder he hasn't snuffed it already. Now Bowles has told him he's got to pack it in. They don't want the job of looking after them and George thinks they'll bump them off. He's cut up to blazes."

Bella stood the iron up slowly, the lead swinging dangerously back and forth in the ceiling light socket. They were both upset and she well understood Tom's frustration. She was not the only woman working day-to-day at home who had enjoyed watching the team move up and down beside the homes ploughing the fields in between, the small, tough old man walking tirelessly in their wake turning the huge chestnut horses about with a word or two. If she'd just made a pot of tea when he was at the end of a row, she would often take him out a big mug of it. He only carried cold tea in his knapsack for his lunch break, and much appreciated a warm drink in between.

"We were all relieved, weren't we, when George was allowed to keep those horses when he retired. How cruel to simply take them back and get rid of them now he's finding it too much. There aren't many of those great horses about now – all off to slaughter. They were all Suffolk Punches round here when I was a girl," she said, wistfully.

"I feel guilty driving that blessed tractor, like it's all the cause of this happening," Tom spoke glumly.

"That's progress," said Bella. "Like this dreadful iron affair. I swear I'd rather go back to heating my old irons on the range. I knew where I was then. This newfangled arrangement will either electrocute me or have me falling off the chair trying to plug it in!"

Tom walked off to the kitchen to put the kettle on. He wasn't listening to talk about ironing. Bella followed him. "You've not a lot of gardening on this time of year Tom. Could you help George out for now, till someone comes up with something else?" she asked.

"I don't know a blessed thing about those damn-great animals," he answered.

"Well, you like them, don't you? George will show you the rest. You could at least do some of the heavy fetch and carry, just for now, and help George out of a hole. Well, it's the only thing I can think of to help." she continued uncertainly.

Tom ticked over, leaning against the sink while the kettle boiled. "I'll slip up to George now," he said deciding, "See what he says."

Two hours later he was back, swinging through the door much more his usual self. Bella was upstairs putting the ironing away in the enormous pine chest of drawers. He noticed that the potatoes on the stove were about to boil over. He called upstairs "Potatoes are boiling over, gal." He knew she'd be pleased he'd noticed. She hated the mess they made and she'd be down to turn them off or low, or something. You never knew, they might be cooked by now. She scuttled

110

through the stair-door giving him one of her 'looks' (he called them) on the way to the kitchen, but he was concentrating on his successful afternoon.

"Both of us went to Bowles and told him we'd carry on in our own time between us if I could use the tractor to shift the muck to stack in the sugar beet field. He looked pretty relieved, I thought. He doesn't really want the job of having them put down, and agreed almost straight away. George is a sight happier, I can tell you."

Bella gave a sigh of relief. "Perhaps the other men will give a hand when word gets round," she said.

"When I get the hang of handling those horses, I can go and let them out on my own, save George turning out all the time. Bella, I stood by that Fancy today and George got me to lift one of her hind legs. She wouldn't put it down when I let go, kept drawing it up under her. I thought she wanted to give me a kick, but George said she didn't want to put it down on me. She wanted to be sure I was standing out of the way. I gave her a bit of a brush, then Hector. George just spoke to them and they moved over.

Bella laughed, "You look as if you're in love, Tom. That tractor's going to get short shrift now. You'll be taking those horses up and down again next!"

"Come the spring, they can be out all day, when the fields are dry and a bit greener. It'll be easier then for George," he said.

Tom went off to wash his hands looking very pleased with himself, Bella thought.

Later, when they were both sitting down to eat, Bella said: "I hate to remind you Tom, but we'll have to choose a chicken to kill tomorrow. The darkest one with the wonky comb is the biggest. They've all stopped laying now, I've got only a couple of dozen eggs in isinglass, then I'll have to use that dried stuff."

Tom dared to ask, "Are you going to swap with next door like you did last year?"

"Yes, Annie and I think it's the only way after that awful

111

year when we were all trying to eat Betsy. We'll swap chickens day after tomorrow. Will you kill and pluck tomorrow, then?" Bella wouldn't let her neighbours kill their chicken, she wanted to be sure a proper job of it was made for her hen.

That took the shine off the day a bit, thought Tom. He hoped Bella didn't guess how much he disliked killing a chicken. She was such a dab hand at drawing and paunching game, but he hated his part of the bargain.

It made him smile, though, when he remembered last year; the women soberly exchanging chickens. Each woman solemnly advanced to the fence bearing aloft her dead, plucked chicken, secured by its feet, in a strong, work-woman's fist. Tom watched, as the tune from 'High Noon' rattled uncontrollably through his head. He would even have risked humming a bar or two, if he hadn't been tone-deaf, of course. Huh! He bet Bella would again comment that she thought her bird would be more tender than Annie's. He'd better agree!

Chapter 23

Betty's stepbrother Joe struggled to extract Grannie's shopping from the panniers on the sides of his motorbike and took the two bags into the kitchen. He was determined to get her larder well-stocked with food before the shop closed for days over Christmas.

"That's the lot, Gran. I've kept the soap away from the tea and sugar; it's in with the candles."

"Did you get me Womans Own?" asked Grannie, who'd had an equally difficult struggle to heave herself out of her old chair.

"Yes, but Mrs Brown says sorry, no crab paste, only bloater. OK?"

"Thanks, Joseph. I'll use some of that there tea and make us a pot. Can you stay, boy?"

'Boy' was now forty years old, but had ceased telling his Gran to give over and stop calling him boy. Ever since tea had come off ration in October, a delighted Grannie proceeded to make tea every couple of hours or so; it was what she called her luxury. And what did Gran do with all those candles, Joe wondered? Candles were always on her list.

As he sat, a thought sidled into his mind. He bet, what with all that tea she was brewing, she was having to burn the midnight candles in the privy. It was not to be recommended that a lady well in her 70s, should sit in an outside draught at all hours of a December day or night, but he well knew from past experience that he couldn't question her on her 'habits'. They were hers and her business and not for him or any other person, to question. He made a mental note to talk to Nurse Crombie and ask her to call in on his Gran as she went past on her rounds.

Grannie put the lid on her capacious brown teapot, happy to be sharing this brew with her much loved grandson. "I made a cake today, boy, a sponge cake. My mum, your great granny," (she always included the relationship when she spoke of the family) "said I had too heavy hands to make a light sponge. Well, I made a good 'un today," she said with satisfaction.

"You're a phenomenon, Gran."

Grannie stopped and hovered like a kestrel before the swoop. "What's that then?" she asked, a belligerent manner covering her uncertainty.

"You're something remarkable."

"That's all right, then." She smiled up at Joe, seeing only kindness in his open face. Content, she turned away and cut him a wide slice of Victoria sponge liberally filled with raspberry jam. "There, that's better'n coke."

"Coke?" Joe didn't know where Grannie got to in her head, sometimes.

"Kitty, my sister, your Great Aunt Kitty, used to eat coke. I told her, no goodness in it, but she said she liked the crunch. Always a bit cranky, mind. P'raps she needed a bit of something extra in her diet, wartime an' all. More use'n they old cigarettes, o' course. Makes more sense." Joe, waiting (in vain, this time) for Gran to tell him 'them cigarettes'll pickle your innards', simply shook his head. He suspected that she saved up funny little anecdotes just to amuse him each week and enjoyed telling him these stories. Whether they were true or not, he always endeavoured to look suitably shocked or impressed. He felt rather sorry for his poor old Gran, on her own for nearly half her lifetime. She must be finding it harder to cope as time went by, but she maintained an outward toughness, pride lending her a straight stance with head held high.

He worried for her on her own like this, but he knew she would not appreciate any comments he might make about her moving away from her own home, even if he asked her to come and live with him. He stayed as late as he could, sitting with her. He banked up her fire before he left and wished he could do more.

Grannie sat in her favourite old chair by the fire watching the flames draw patterns in the soot on the fireback, contemplating whether to make another cup of tea as a nightcap or not. A phenomenon that's what Joseph said she was. That meant Special and it made her smile. Then her eyes fell on the magazine and she stretched to retrieve it from the floor. Settling further into her chair, she flicked over the pages to find the latest news on the Royal family.

Comfortable now, she reached over to the table, selected from the greaseproof paper one of the new, pristine white candles and contentedly began to chew on it.

Chapter 24

Christmas Day started at 5 a.m. for Jack and Peggy, just as it did last year. Alex and Rosie shot into their bedroom, Rosie jumped up and down on the spot lost for words, then scooted back to her little bed for her stocking in which remained only the orange and apple and dragged it behind her back to Jack's side of the big bed. He leaned over and pulled her, still clutching her stocking, into the warm bed. Her toes were so chilled from the cold lino, her little feet were a shock against his warm legs. Alex was more eloquent and shouted with excitement as he bundled in on top of Peggy who groaned and came to. Her voice deep and slow with the residue of sleep, she wished them all a Merry Christmas, then sat up in bed and smiled lazily down at Jack as the children shouted "Merry Christmas" back.

"Just as well we're awake early today – I'll take these two with me when I pick Tom up this morning," said Jack ruefully making the best of the early waking.

"Will you manage them as well as those big animals," asked Peggy doubtfully.

"I think we'll all enjoy it," said Jack. "Tom and I together should be able to keep kids and animals separated I should think!"

Jack, on hearing at the packing shed that Tom was doing the horses for George on Christmas Day, offered to pick him up in the car and help him at the stables.

Alex and Rosie were enchanted to be given such a Christmas treat, and Alex gleefully took on the task of filling the empty buckets with water. Jack slung a horse blanket over the huge pile of hay in the rack above Fancy and Hector, then lifted Rosie on top of it, well out of the way, and tied a rein round her. He mollified her with, "Just like the horses, Rosie." Looking down and watching the men put halters on the horses was very new and interesting to Rosie, who forgot her restriction – and the prickles in the hay – for the moment.

Tom, glancing at Rosie, started to chant, "Away in a Manger – but-not-for-long," but no one could stand tone deaf Tom trying to sing and Jack told him to shut up or he would frighten the horses. One day, when the men were more used to handling them, the children would be allowed to ride them out to the field – straddling their short legs across the horses' wide backs, while the men lead them – but not yet.

Once the horses were safely away, Jack lifted a tousled Rosie down from her perch whereupon she set off at great speed to dabble in the water buckets before one of them caught up with her. Quickly Jack gave her a trug full of brushes and horse combs and tried not to look as she did her best to brush and comb her hair with them. She'd have to be upended and topped and tailed later. Right now they all had to set about swilling down the stable channels and yard to work up a good appetite for their Christmas dinner through the cold, clear morning.

Peggy, at home with a clear run through till nearly dinner time, wrapped silver threepenny bits to push into the Christmas pudding. She would watch to make sure each child found one and didn't swallow it. While keeping her eye on the cooking chicken, she realised the oven was losing heat and found, without much surprise, what had become a local tradition at Christmas; the electricity, overloaded with all that day's cooking, had cut off once again. She was now up to this one and took the whole tray of food out of the Jackson and put it in the range oven alongside the fire in the living room to finish. The pudding, made when the hens were laying and eggs were plentiful, had already been steamed for seven hours and had only to be left on top of the range for another half hour. She'd also better find the candles while she had a minute – the electricity usually came back before dark, but no one was ever sure.

117

With one last check to see everything was all right, she lifted the cat off her chair. Sitting down, she slipped off her shoes, pushing her toes into the rag rug she'd pegged the winter before last. The warmth-dazed cat focussed on her with half-closed eyes and, warning her with a small chirrup, jumped up onto her lap. This was a present to herself; time on her own to dream a little before they all came trooping back in.

Chapter 25

Things weren't going quite so swimmingly in the bakery household however. They were faced with each other for the day with nothing to preoccupy or distract them and the silence was heavy and oppressive. No peace and contentment here, only hostility and despair.

Sally scraped round the edge of the kitchen, hair tumbled and dressing gown thrown on, getting ever more het up as she shakily lit the grill. Peter edged around the other side of the room, keeping clear, quietly making a cup of coffee, with the fervent hope it would all go away. Farcically, they had wished each other "Happy Christmas" in echoing dull voices as they met, as if by chance, in the kitchen that morning.

Keeping the lid hard on it so it wouldn't get out was not going to work. Jim had (just) honoured his promise to Sally that he would let her break the news her way. The day was going to be anything but happy. The tension had built strongly, it wouldn't take much to snap.

"Peter," ventured Sally.

"What?" He stared at her. He could not know whether he was beginning to shake from his sudden anger or the sickening fear which had been stalking him for so long.

Sally froze at the look on Peter's florid face. She stood dumbly, her hands involuntarily lifting away from her body in a hopeless expression.

"WHAT," the word shot abruptly from Peter, his face suffused with red. He felt pushed into a confrontation he had been trying so hard to avoid.

"Peter," she put out a hand as if to try to calm him. "I have to tell you." She took a big breath, "There's a man I've been seeing…"

"No, I don't believe it – not you, you wouldn't!" Then, "Who?" as if the word, hard said, would more quickly extract the answer.

Sally slumped down into a chair feeling its side-edge – a strong support, "Jim Macaulay," she whispered.

He stood, shocked at first, unable to comprehend, then, "You rotten little cheat," he exploded. "It's unbelievable – how could you?" He was moving fast across the room, his face ugly, thrust forward, eyes dark with threat. He leaned across the table, each hand gripping an edge while he glared into her face.

Frightened, she leaned back in the chair as far as she could get and looked up at him. With his face hard above her she couldn't move, mustn't move. If she moved a muscle, she was sure he would hit her. Shocked at the thought that he could do this, she sat frozen for a long, suspended moment.

The breath sighed out of him. His hands slowly unclenched. "You've gone mad – I don't believe you." He looked at her more searchingly, "Why?"

Achingly slowly the tension subsided as Peter waited for an answer.

She lifted her head a fraction and tried to say with a little dignity, "You and I haven't been getting on for ages. You took me for-granted for a long while before I woke up to it. I felt all you wanted out of me was for me to work for you in the bakery."

"For US, Sally, and it's not true."

"NOT for us," she came back just as emphatically. I didn't want just work and money and tiredness at the end of it, day after day, I told you this! All you could say was that I knew what I was getting in to when I married you! Why did you marry me?"

He looked at her as if she was indeed mad. "Surely you knew I love you, Sally. I thought you loved me. We make our life together, you and I."

Guilt and sadness weighed her down and she went on more quietly, "When I married you, Peter, I had stars in my eyes. I couldn't see the future was day-to-day dull routine – it shouldn't have been! We were so young – you made us an old couple before our time. It started when you came back from the War. It changed you, it was bound to, but you shut me out. I waited, hoping you'd speak about it and let me in to help, or that it would come right in time. It didn't. You were so bad tempered – morose. You didn't want to share."

Peter stood, thunderstruck, then, "We've talked about all that before…"

"Yes," Sally shot back, "but nothing changed!" and then more quietly, "Do you remember when the van wouldn't go, the day you were going to take me to West Mersea?"

"But you understood…"

"It was the last straw!"

"And you bloody-well went off with another man because of THAT?" He started to pound a fist on the table.

"NO, you fool! Because of all that led up to it!" Her temper rose at last and forced back her despair at his seeming inability to grasp what she was trying to explain. "Did we ever discuss why we didn't have children? No," (before he had a chance to answer) "you didn't want them, did you. It would have taken me away from looking after you and that wretched business you are married to. When I brought up the subject, you skirted round it. Hid behind whatever was happening then. Said we'd think about it soon. Anything to shut me up!"

He felt chastened by her counter-attack and looked down and away from her as she carried on, "You were prepared to go on as we were, going nowhere because you just didn't want to see anything else. Well, I'd had enough and you didn't listen, just so long as things always went the way you wanted them to."

She sank once more back into the chair. "Jim came along just at that time – I didn't fall for him on purpose, you know, it just happened!"

"Fall for him! You cheating…! What exactly is that supposed to mean?"

With a big effort she faced him with the inevitable outcome. "It means I am going to go and live with him, Peter."

"And leave me?" It was said, dragged from him at last, as he tried to make sense of it all.

She had no more energy, "Yes, Peter. I'm sorry."

She got up slowly and walked out and upstairs to what was now her bedroom and shut the door. Then, turning again, she locked it. She'd keep out of his way for the rest of this awful day. Christmas! She needed Jim so badly. Though so near, just along the road, he was busy with a pre-Christmas dinner drinks session when a lot of the men slipped in for a quick one. If he knew she'd finally told Peter, she was sure he'd be with her nonetheless. He'd been so worried when she begged him to leave it to her. Peter had been close to hitting her, she knew, but it would have been much worse if Jim had been there with her to face him – and unfair to Peter, she thought. She lay on her back, staring up at the ceiling. Now it was out in the open, she wanted to be away from here with Jim – how could she wait? With Peter downstairs, she could not even telephone across to Jim to let him know what had happened, but she would pack a case in the morning and ring him then. In a mixture of anguish and hope, the tears came at last.

Rousing, Peter stared round the empty kitchen and his eyes fell on the small, naked chicken. It had been sitting on the table since Sally had dumped it there that morning from the cupboard where it had been hanging, a pathetic accent on a Christmas meaningless for them both. He picked it up and threw it at the wall, then stormed off to his bakery, now his refuge.

Sitting in the covered way on a ledge between the kitchen and the bakery was a small selection of drinks, he had only yesterday hopefully brought home for Sally and himself. With a grimace, he now acknowledged the pretence of this show of unity at Christmas. As he marched past, his hand shot out for the bottle of whisky which fell neatly into his large hand – he'd damned-well drink on his own!

Hunkering down with the bottle in the old chair he occasionally used between jobs here, he felt more at home than he had felt for a long time in that house. He wasn't going back to fetch a glass either, he'd drink from the bottle.

What did bloody women want anyway? Why had this happened to him? He'd always been faithful, looked after her. She'd regret this when she realised and came to her senses... Of course, it was that scheming sod up the road. He knew how to seduce a young inexperienced woman like Sally. Easy for him, an older man who had been married before. Living on his own, with no one to answer to, and nothing to lose in sweet-talking an innocent girl like Sally. And then she falls straight into his lap! Sorry. Sorry? Was that it? He hadn't had a chance yet to get to grips with it and try to talk some sense into Sally. Oh, Sally! He was still in shock.

With nothing in his stomach but a quickly made cup of coffee this morning, he took his first drink. Settling more heavily in his comfortable chair and automatically lifting the bottle as if to punish himself, he struggled to understand the day's events.

Thinking, miserable, while the edges of the day dulled and blurred as the bottle emptied, his last thought was, what a sodding Christmas this turned out to be. Then alcohol blanked out self-pity and he slumped where he lay in the chair, the bottle, less than a third in it falling from his loosening grasp to roll, unheeded across the tiled floor.

Up in her room, Sally alternately lay on the bed and fretted about how she would get away in the morning, carefully unlocking the door, and crept to the top of the stairs to listen for Peter. Where was he? If she managed to slip out past him, where would she go? The pub was full of people coming and going through the day with lengthier opening hours than usual. She could not just turn up and walk through that door as if nothing was amiss or hide her white, tear-streaked face from the curious in the saloon and announce to Jim that she had left Peter at last. Nor could she walk the distance to her parent's home and coolly announce that she had come for Christmas dinner, and without Peter. Her mother had made their disapproval of Sally's infidelity very plain. Desperate as she was, she could not face unravelling it all now, with them. No, she would have to wait for one more day.

All right, it was out in the open now, the awful words said. Let Peter get over the initial shock and cool down a bit before she faced him in the morning. She had felt so sorry for Peter, even while she was cutting him with the truth. What if it had been he who had found another woman? Would she really have been as uncaring as she supposed? She recognised these last regretful thoughts for what they were – part of the aftermath of the upsetting scenes downstairs such a short while ago. There would be no return to her life with Peter, of that she was sure. She simply felt an overwhelming relief that the words had been said at last.

Now, looking back, she realised she had wanted to change a lot in her life long before Jim had happened by that day. They had stopped sharing conversation and interests outside the bakery for a long time. For her it hadn't been enough, then Jim had come along and everything changed. Poor Peter!

Chapter 26

Jim woke with an intense headache on Boxing Day. What with worrying quietly all the time about the situation between him and Sally and trying to keep up the appearance of the jolly 'mine host' at Christmas, he was treading a rocking tightrope.

First, he had been well stretched to cope with yesterday's rush of customers just before midday. Then a lot of them went on drinking long after they'd promised their wives they would be home promptly for the biggest dinner of the year. He'd had to use all his tact to shut up shop. Didn't they know how well off they were, these men who took their wives so for granted? Once he and Sally were free to be off on their own to start again, he'd be so appreciative of a good home life once more – as soon as she'd told Peter! The urge rose again simply to follow his impulse, to disregard her entreaties that she alone should face Peter. Only too aware that he must contain his impatience, he nevertheless wondered how much longer he could tolerate this feeling of helpless drift. If he found she'd said nothing after today, when she would have a good opportunity, then he would insist they face Peter together and get it over with. After that, they could start afresh.

It was just light at 6 a.m. when Jim tumbled downstairs, made a cup of strong coffee and found Pip curled down in a tight ball in his corner by the stove.

"Hello, old boy, good job they can't put weight on you with all the crisps you're offered in the bar. Do you want to go out?"

The thin little black lurcher crept out of his basket and stretched back and forth before gently padding to the back door and the garden.

"We'll go for a walk – it'll clear my head." It would kill time too, he thought, and he'd feel more awake when he went over to face the situation with Sally. He'd give Pip a much-needed stretch and he could work out a strategy (if there was any in this situation) at the same time.

Deciding to take the van and park near the top of their favourite field this crisp Boxing Day morning, he bundled Pip in the back. He slowed down to a crawl past the bakery to see if there was any movement yet, but the house seemed still and quiet. He felt in a strange limbo, couldn't go forward, couldn't go back – but it had gone on long enough!

Chapter 27

Jim wasn't the only one waking with a sore head. Peter felt lifeless, stiff with cold as he surfaced in his old chair. He heaved himself up and looked down at the bottle on the floor. "Oh God!" and clutched his head. It was a long time since he had had a drink, let alone nearly a full bottle of Scotch. Where was the wretched woman? He groaned. How could she do this to him? She was his wife; he'd lock her in the house, wouldn't let her go off like that. She had no right!

He heaved himself to his feet and stood swaying till the room steadied, then lurched through the porch area, where a van creeping past outside caught his eye. "That oily swine, sliding by, with his nose stuck out looking for my wife!" he said aloud while rage swamped his fuddled head. He fumbled to open the door and lunged down the path. He couldn't wait to get his fists round Macaulay, but he missed the latch with his shaking hands and by the time he pulled himself upright, Jim's van had disappeared.

Full of vengeance, he was about to jerk at the door latch again when he saw his rabbiting gun. Well, he'd shot a few rats in his time with that and anger ousting coherent thought, he grasped a handful of cartridges and flung it into the van with the shotgun.

He knew where Macaulay walked his dog. He couldn't believe his luck; he could tackle him away from prying eyes and his bloody customers! There'd be a damned-sight different outcome to the one Macaulay was planning, he'd see to that! Macaulay would have to listen to threats of what he'd do to him if he didn't keep away from his wife with a gun poked in his face.

Peter found Jim's van and parked his own out of sight.

Quietly, his confidence growing, he loaded the weapon and tucked it under his arm. Reassured that he now had the means to take control of the situation, if it came to it, he peered over the stile where he thought Jim had gone. Jim, head down, agitated in thought, was walking fast. Peter had lost a bit of time, but if he caught up stealthily, he would then have the advantage. He so wanted to get his hands on him! Pip was loping along well ahead of Jim at the edge of a field. There were a few rabbits giving the gazehound a good run. She could see far and ran after any game that moved, enjoying the chase. Peter, trying to walk fast and catch up, was hampered by also trying to tread quietly to surprise his quarry.

Jim slipped through the next gap in the hedge and Peter could only see his old green hat above the line of thicket. By the time Peter reached the hedge and looked cautiously over, Jim had made a left turn and was walking towards Bella's place. This was to be a short walk, he thought, or was he intending to cross the road below Bella's and call in on Sally's people? Maybe Sally went there last night! No, No, he wouldn't have it! They planned to be off together and he wouldn't have a chance to do a thing about it. He saw the hated shape about to disappear as it marched smartly to the corner of the building at the top of Bella's garden and he couldn't bear to see his chance go. He lifted the rifle in a desperate reflex and squeezed the trigger.

Chapter 28

Bella always looked forward to Boxing Day. This, for her and Tom, was their family day. There would be more exchanges of presents, which gave the children an extra treat after the excitement of Christmas Day itself. It had become a tradition that there would be a large ham for dinner, followed by another Christmas pudding. They could all manage just one more of those.

Tom came home with their share of the Pig Club meat each year – half a pig. She had always been given a whole head to make brawn though, since some of the housewives squeamishly refused part of the head with their share. Tom particularly enjoyed it, eaten with vinegar and chunks of bread for his supper. She would simmer the head and trotters with herbs and seasoning in her huge preserving pan, cut the good meat into chunks when it cooled and set it all back in the jelly. Then, although she had a cool north facing cupboard to store her meats and whatever else came her way within those rationing days, she still had to bring the brawn to a simmer every other day to keep it good to eat, before setting it out on the windowsill to cool and gel all over again.

After the ham had been baked with cloves dotted in the squared scoring, Tom lifted it out to cool. He stropped the worn blade of the carving knife on the steel and began to carve thick rounds of moist meat and lay each piece on the long meat plate. The pile grew, a thick, creamy blush of fat smiling round the rim of each succulent slice. Tom leaned across to breathe in the aromatic wisps, still rising from it. Offering Bella a slice from his knife, he raised another small slice slowly to his mouth to 'test' the flavour of the ham – another tradition – one which made Bella smile.

While watching him carve, Bella set the table and opened her jars of pickled beetroot and chutney. He offered her a glass of sherry but, unused to drink, she refused, determined to keep a clear head at least till after dinner or she wouldn't get the meal on the table. There were carols on the wireless and Tom built a good fire in the black range for the family to gather round when they had eaten. The little room gleamed in the firelight, the polished furniture shone, the handed-down decorations once more in place, testimony to Bella's sure hand.

Soon there was the sound of fast-running feet and hammering on the door and William and Barry flung themselves inside giving their grandparents big, excited hugs, followed by a cheerful Elsie and Alan bearing armfuls of presents. Jack's little car stopped on the path for the second time that day. Earlier he had called with some extra chairs. Now Jack and Alex with Peggy towing Rosie, caught up with all the others taking their coats off in the kitchen.

They settled with drinks and mince pies before their dinners while Bella and Tom worked out with Alan and Jack where they were going to put the chairs, boxes and anything else they could rustle up to sit themselves upon. Alex was enchanted to see they each had a cracker. Rosie was about to find out that they had a loud bang.

With Rosie now strapped into the old highchair that had always seemed to be about at her grandparents, the boys, feeling important on their own small table, were allowed to pull the crackers. Relaxed, replete, having just helped to polish off the second Christmas pudding, a much louder bang than they expected made them all jump and Rosie cry. She had just got used to all the fuss they had been making of her each time a cracker banged.

Tom looked up sharply. "That was close. There's usually some young shaver with more time off than sense shooting at anything that moves."

Jack grinned, "I reckon they get bored indoors all Christmas Day with the old folk," then caught Bella's eye and reddened.

Alan went to the door and looked about. "Gone now, whoever it was. The rabbits don't seem to be too bad right now. I could bag some myself before going back to work – they'll come as a change after all the Christmas food." He shut the door again, and took William and Barry's Meccano into the warm room to see what he could make with the boys, but they wanted to get their coats and boots on and tear off out into the garden. "Shove off then you two, it'll do you good – I think," he said as they bundled out of the door and across the open grass path at a gallop.

William, always the one in front with his longer legs, pushed both feet together in an abrupt halt leaving Barry nearly cannoning into his back, and stared. Through the half-open wooden door on the apron yard of the pig sty sprawled two long legs ending in large boots. They didn't move. The boys edged forward and gingerly pushed the door wider. A tall man lay on his back spread-eagled across the pig trough, very still, his unseeing face turned to the sky in a seemingly uncomfortable state. The boys backed away and turning tail together, raced back to the kitchen door.

Chapter 28 – Continued

Bella and Elsie had just got up to go into the kitchen. Bella was keen to hear how Elsie was getting on at her job with the solicitors and said they might as well wash up as not while they talked. Bella had just put on her pinafore to protect her good dress, when the two boys were back through the door like they'd been let out of school.

"There's a man in the piggery and he doesn't look very well – he's on the floor and not moving at all." William looked uncertainly from one to the other of the women.

"He's fallen over right out of his hat," put in Barry.

Bella, with lips pressed together, shot a sideways look at Elsie – one of their games?

Tom called from his chair, "I'll go; I thought this would be too good to last." He thought the boys seemed too worried to be putting them through one of their smile-straining jokes. He strode to the door with the two youngsters jostling behind him and wondered what it was all about. Seconds later he came running back to say that old Macaulay was toes-up in the pig trough. "Out cold," he said.

The whole household erupted, Bella taking time to run upstairs to fetch a blanket, while everyone ran back up the path to see what they could do. Only Rosie still sat in her highchair where she'd been chewing on a biscuit and watching the women in the kitchen. Now her world had gone very quiet all of a sudden.

"Blahted earwigs," she said quite distinctly, but no one was there to hear her.

Tom knelt down beside Jim and gently felt his neck for a pulse. "He's alive, anyway. He must have hit his head when he fell. Give me that blanket love, I'll try to get it round him as best I can, but we shouldn't move him, they say."

"I'll get to the phone box," said Jack and ran off to turn his car round to take it the short ride up the road to the phone box standing on the verge. It was while Tom and Alan were trying to wrap Jim up but not move him too much, that they found the blood. It was oozing from beneath his right shoulder. Blood! The three boys nudged each other closer, to see more. Quickly, Elsie led them away, while Peggy, suddenly remembering Rosie, spun round to run back for her. She had begun to yell and struggle in her chair.

Jim was still unconscious when the ambulance men lifted him into their vehicle, much to the fascination of the children.

"What a strange thing to happen," said Bella.

"What on earth was he doing there I wonder?" returned Peggy.

"That shot we heard – Macaulay wasn't in the way of that surely – was he?" It had suddenly struck Tom that this could have been so.

They all trooped back into the house and Elsie put the kettle on – a cup of tea always put things in better perspective. "I've never seen him with any family or relatives at all," mused Alan. "I'll phone up and check on things later tonight. I'll let you know if they tell me how he is." It wasn't long after that that the family went home, all somewhat subdued, and Tom and Bella, as always after a family get-together, found the house settle and go very quiet again. Poor old Jim Macaulay. It had put a bit of a damper on the day.

"Well, this has been a rare sort of Boxing Day," said Tom standing thoughtfully in the bedroom in his vest, his best socks held up with striped suspenders. Bella hid a smile; it wouldn't do for Tom to catch her amused, but she always thought he looked like a lost boy whenever he stood like that, uncertain, with his hair tousled and standing on end. "Like a Christmas robin thrown from his nest," she couldn't resist saying aloud.

"What are you on about woman," he said, one suspicious

133

eye on her as he sorted out his pyjamas.

"Are you going to stand there all night, Thomas Whitley while I shiver in bed or are you going to get in here and warm me up?" Thomas Whitley was not a man to be told twice when it came to a cuddle with the woman of his life and he thumped happily into bed pulling Bella close.

No one had given a thought to whether his lurcher had been with Jim Macaulay, or where he was.

Chapter 29

Jack called in to see his mother the next day with Alex and Rosie in tow. He and Peggy had talked of little else since the wounded man had been taken to hospital. He had stopped by at Elsie's on the way and Alan had told him that Jim was now conscious but that the shoulder was sore and bruised from a gunshot wound. All being well, he'd be home in a couple of weeks.

"Who the heck hit old Macaulay, then Mum?" asked Jack. "What a peculiar accident."

Bella cast him a warning look, then said, "Have you children seen the kittens yet? Missy has four on top of the coal bunker. Go and have a look, you two, while you still have your coats on." They needed no second bidding. "Don't worry, they can't reach her," added Bella. "Have you heard any gossip in that packing shed lately, Jack?"

"Well..."

"Uh huh, so there's been some goings on. I don't know how long or how much, but I did see him with Sally in town not so long ago and they looked very cosy to me."

"Peter did it?" Jack sounded incredulous. "Come on Mum. You've been reading too many detective books! Things like that don't happen round here."

"Pinching other people's husbands and wives happens everywhere Jack. Where have you been? It's only lucky the children wanted to go out and play yesterday. If it had been colder or raining, they'd have stayed in and who knows what might have happened to the poor man. He could have died out there while no one knew where he was."

Was it possible that Peter had actually shot Jim Macaulay? Jack wondered. Another thought crossed his mind. "Mum, may I leave those two with you for a while? Someone ought to go along and just check on the pub. The door ought to be locked, but I could put up a notice so that the regulars won't try to break it down at opening time." He grinned. "They'll have to do without till Jim gets back."

"Oh, good idea Jack," and then, "What about the dog? I haven't seen a whisker of him, but I bet he was with Jim when he started out. He'd not have gone for a walk on his own. I think its name is 'Pip' from what I can recall, it goes with a slight little dog like that. Keep a look-out while you're there Jack, though I expect the police will be about there soon enough."

Bella passed him a big piece of brown paper to write a message and then, just as he was leaving, ran out with two ham bones from the previous day, to give to Pip, if he could find him.

"That's all I can spare at the moment," she said apologetically. "He's a shy dog and I doubt you'll get near him even if he does show up while you're there, but you can leave these and a drop of water near the back door just in case."

"I won't be long," said Jack and waved himself off out of the five bar gate and onto the Harwich Road. He bowled along the three or four miles of empty road without once having to use his brakes and turned straight in and up the gravel pathway to the back of the pub. He tried the door at the front and then walked round to the back. Both were secure, though Jim didn't always remember to lock up when he went out.

He looked around. There was no sign of the dog. He took the bag which Bella had given him and with a lot of rustling, tipped one of the bones out by the back step. There was a tap in the back yard with an empty dog bowl nearby, so he filled it up with clean water and called encouragingly. He didn't expect the dog to respond, but slowly a delicately pointed black nose inched round the side of the wooden shed. Jack carried on placing the bowl of water down and talking softly. He wasn't a great animal lover, not like most of the women in his life, even including two year old Rosie, but he would hate to see one lost or hungry and he would do his best. Peggy would know what to do for the dog, once he had caught it and taken it home. He sat down and rolled a cigarette. The dog, seeing him settled and unworried, crept nearer. The smell of the tobacco was familiar to him and he felt reassured. Jack puffed away unconcerned, watching the creature, shy and delicate as a deer, sniff all round the bone before lifting it gingerly and skipping away. Jack hadn't moved. It would have been easier with a bluff, friendly old Labrador, he thought. Try and keep Bob's away. This one, though, could test his patience.

The cigarette was gone, but the dog was back again. He held the second bone out to the wispy, frail-looking lurcher. Jack was glad that he was not particularly wary of men, what with his master running a pub and taking him on rabbit-hunting expeditions, often in other men's company. Just as the dog's arched neck stretched out as far as it could to take the second bone, Jack stuck a quick finger under the collar and drew the light body towards him, still talking gently. He folded his other arm along its chest and the mild-natured dog subsided against Jack, who softly put him into the front seat of the car. The troubles that beset the dog's master would not be so easily solved, he thought, as he made his way back to pick up the children. If they made a great fuss of the little dog and Peggy wanted to keep it for the time being, he would not object. It might be good for the two little ones to look after someone's dog for a while. He'd call in to the police station in Ardleigh and ask them if this would be OK. They'd know where Pip was if anyone should happen to turn up to claim him. Did Jim have any relatives he wondered?

When Jack called in at the Police Station, Paul, the Constable at the desk looked relieved to hear that Jack would take the lurcher home. He'd had a few dogs tied up in the station over the years and it was the devil's own job just to get close enough to read an address on their collars, if they wore one, that was. He knew most of the dogs about here. One or two had chased him along the road on his bicycle. He wondered why people kept dogs, or any animal that wasn't a useful one. They seemed to cause no end of trouble and heartache.

"Thanks, Jack," he called as Jack went out of the door. He picked up his pen and made a note on the pad in front of him. There was a lot more in this to get to the bottom of, than the fate of Jim's dog. One of the officers was with Jim right now, trying to find out how he came to be shot, the first time such a thing had happened around here.

Chapter 30

Benny the postman knocked on Sally's door. Sally opened the door a small crack, thinking to take a bulky letter from Benny. It was enough for him to see she was very unhappy and, unusually for her, hair uncombed, face blotched, eyes puffy. He'd known her since they were children at school. "Whatever's the matter, love? You don't look too well. Where's Peter – is he OK?"

"Yes, he's fine," she lied. "I have a bit of a cold, could be flu coming," she added shortly. She needed to keep her wits about her. She'd heard Peter starting the van yesterday and, looking out cautiously from the bedroom window, had seen him practically throw his gun into the back. He'd looked awful and it was clear from the state of him that he'd slept in his clothes and must have been feeling as dreadful as he looked.

Worried, she'd dressed with haste and without bothering to lift the phone — she so badly wanted to see Jim — she'd run along to the Wooden Fender. He wasn't there. She had spent a day watching and waiting in between phoning the pub. Nothing. She was at her wits end wondering and worrying; he wouldn't leave her without a word unless something had happened. She must stay put so he knew where she was.

This morning, she felt lifeless and her hand shook as she took the letter from Benny and made to close the door. "You've not heard about your neighbour, then," said Benny, always ready to pass on and hear the local news. He was speaking about Jim, of course, her only neighbour.

Sally involuntarily opened the door wider, her face sharper, eyes intent. "What about him?" she asked quickly.

"He's been shot. In hospital now, but they say he's over the worst and will be back home within a fortnight. Shot, though. How on earth did that happen?"

Sally was aghast, "No, oh no, not Jim," she said before she could recover.

"Yes, old Macaulay, but don't worry too much, love, he'll be all right. Some mad young devil with an air rifle I expect. Caught him by accident when he was out walking; from quite a distance, they say. Paul says they're going to have to go round and look at all the guns now to see which one was fired. That'll take some time; a lot of us have them for rabbits and such. I wonder there's any game left about here."

Sally's colour washed slowly back into her face as Benny talked. At least she knew where Jim was. She couldn't, wouldn't, think beyond that for now. What a mess! Did anything ever go to plan? Get dressed, that was the first thing. She must go and see Jim in hospital but the wretched bus didn't go till 2 o'clock. She'd just have to wait... and fret.

It didn't take Einstein – or even an imported detective from the town – to work out what was going on when Sally finally catapulted into the ward where Jim Macaulay lay.

Jim was curled on his unwounded side, asleep, one arm extended from the bedcover. Sally slowed her frantic pace while her heart squeezed at the sight. He looked so vulnerable. Seeing then, from his relaxed features that he was comfortable and mending, she moved slowly to his side and lifted his hand. As he awoke, and focussed on her face, she bent to plant a kiss firmly on his mouth, and watched his eyes glow with pleasure and relief.

This was when Sergeant Willow returned to Jim Macaulay's bedside with a cup of tea he had begged from the kitchen. He had been waiting for the wounded man to wake.

140

With eyes only for each other, Jim and Sally did not register a policeman's quiet approach round the pulled-back curtain by the bed. Eager to hear exactly what had happened to Jim, she turned to find a chair and found herself instead face to face with the Sergeant. Sighing, he put the cup down on the windowsill and looked beyond Sally to Jim.

"I'm here to try to find out how you came to be shot," Sergeant Willow explained.

"I've no idea." Jim looked blank. "It was an accident, of course." There was no hiding from the Sergeant the feelings between him and Sally, he thought, so, looking up at the policeman, he added: "Sally and I couldn't have kept our secret much longer. We know we're going to have to face it. Then we shall have to get away together as soon as we can."

Sergeant Willow stood up and took his leave with alacrity. What a stroke of luck! He saw at once where his enquiries should be made. He'd saved a lot of time this morning.

The big black Morris rumbled to a halt outside the bakery, but Peter wasn't there. After a whole day's search the police couldn't find him anywhere else either. What's more, Sergeant Willow realised that there wouldn't be any bread baked here for some while and that alone was cause for some dismay. Mrs Brown at her little general store would have to order more batches of that cotton wool stuff they'd 'kissed and blessed', or something, and dared to call bread. It came already wrapped in a packet which squashed like a concertina. When they'd paraded it on television, Mrs Willow had been beguiled enough to present him with a slice, but he couldn't choke it down, not even plastered with some of her plum jam.

No point in waiting about here. The trail was as cold as the ovens inside the place. They would have to spread the search wider. The Sergeant returned to the car and drove off.

Chapter 31

With the report of the shotgun came a slam on Peter's shoulder, force enough to jerk him nearly off balance and loud enough to shock him out of his madness. In his haste to lift the gunstock he hadn't given himself time to set it to his shoulder with careful aim but he had seen that sneaking sod Macaulay reel. He'd certainly hit him!

His balance returned, his heartbeat slowed and the momentary satisfaction that he'd stopped his enemy was replaced by the slow dawning that he might have killed him. He had wanted to stop him, get near enough to lay hands on him and teach him to leave other men's wives alone, but not this. He sank down onto the ground where he stood and desperately tried to go through it in his mind. He breathed deeply, consciously trying to calm himself and think rationally. Macaulay had been hit, he'd veered, listed towards the corner of the building, and then he had gone out of sight. Peter had fired before he'd snugged the gun to his shoulder; hit high. He could have hit him in the head. Yes, he could very well have killed him, and if he had killed him he might hang. How he hated Jim Macaulay. First, he had stolen his wife, and then he'd made him a fugitive.

He sat, head low, cooling down and clearing his thoughts for some while, until he became aware of the dampness of the ground. Cold shivered through him and he was about to stand upright when caution stayed him and he looked round, half bent, to see if there was anyone about. No one. Well it was dinner time on Boxing Day. He shook his head in disgust; he had no idea how had he had come to be in this mess. He would have given anything to be happy at home having his dinner with Sally, living like any normal person.

142

Suddenly fearful, shaking with reaction, he ducked down with the shotgun dragging. He crabbed to the hedgeside, and slipped through heading for Hunting Lane which took a right-angle from the main road. He could not creep back to his van; it only needed one neighbour to come along that road and he would be spotted, and carrying a gun. He'd like to get rid of it, hide it, but here in a flat, open field with just a short hedge for cover it would be so easily found that he might just as well give himself up there and then, and he certainly wasn't about to do that.

Warily, with head bent as low as his big frame would allow, Peter slunk along the straight row of the hedge to the trees which flanked Hunting Lane. Leaving his shotgun on the ground, he strode across a small ditch and clutched the trunk of a half-grown oak to swing a look round. Still no one. He spun back across the ditch to pick up his gun again, then walked out from behind the tree… to face Trixie Langham who had just come down her front path to shut the five-bar gate before she let Tolly out of the stable.

Chapter 32

Caught so unexpectedly, Peter stood transfixed with his gunstock resting on the ground, held loosely by his side. Involuntarily he glanced from side to side as if there might be an escape from Trixie's gaze as she straightened up from the gate latch. Before his wits would function she called, "Fancy seeing you out today – at this time – I thought you'd be toasting your toes by a big fire with Sally." She had thought she'd be the only one on the whole estate who would be trying to amuse herself; endeavouring to get through another Christmas on her own, with only her animals for company. Now here was Peter, so bored he couldn't take a well-earned rest indoors for more than a day without having to get some exercise out on a shoot.

"You know how it is..." he said, trying to sound off-hand (That was all he could manage to say. Oh God, he was in enough trouble without playing at social exchanges). He tried to saunter off while his heart seemed to jump out of his chest, a smile transformed into a grimace as he made to pass by. He felt dishevelled, and was sure she'd soon find out he was in an upset state if he stopped much longer. He had to get away quickly and think.

"Peter, I'm in a bit of a fix," Trixie confessed. "Of all things, I can't clear the bottom of the range fire properly. The wretched pull-push thing at the base won't let me get the fire to draw. I was waiting until I saw someone to ask to give me a hand." She stood looking slightly embarrassed, waiting. She hated above everything having to ask favours like this, but there were some things she found just too hard to manage on her own. This was the great drawback of her way of life which, while she still missed sharing it all with Walter, she otherwise adored.

Peter turned with a helpless sense that this could not really be happening. After shooting a man, for crying out loud, all he wanted to do was give himself a bit of time to work out what he should do now. Walking away just wasn't possible if he wanted to cover up his part in the day's events. If he acted it out and got on with the task, he could then make himself scarce – maybe get as far as Manningtree if he kept off the roads - and catch a train out of this mess before they picked him up. If he acted un-neighbourly, Trixie would easily recall it if she were ever questioned on this dismal business and would add fuel to the speculations.

Trying not to show his weariness, he followed Trixie through the gate and past Tolly who stood watching them in his small paddock. "I like to allow him out to stretch his legs each day, whether I need him for the trap or not," she said. "Just as well it's a bare patch. George says I've to watch the pony's weight."

"Uh, huh," was the only reply from Peter, who nearly bumped into Trixie pushing hard to open the back door into the kitchen. The door had been sticking for some time so that Trixie had got used to it, like a few of the other minor aggravations she worked round on her own. She had learned to concentrate on the important things. The range fire refusing to light at any time of the year was not to be tolerated and certainly not now when the weather was so cold. Peter propped the shotgun up behind the slammed door and followed Trixie into the front room. The surly fire grumbled faintly in the grate, just alight with a low glow. She had managed to augment this miserly comfort with a sulky paraffin heater, now giving off oily fumes in the corner, but it was essential that she have her main cooking and heating source working.

Peter got down on his knees to tug at the damper and found it was stuck fast. It took some manoeuvring and he was quickly running out of patience. He simply wanted to get it done and go. He couldn't believe the situation he was in! He

145

had to batten down his panic every time this realisation forced itself to the surface. He must not become overwhelmed. He just had to keep control.

Trixie hitched herself on the arm of the chair beside the fire and said, "I hope you have some luck with that – you don't look as if you've had any other luck today."

He stopped pushing at the handle and was suddenly still. Without looking up he asked "Oh?" Now what.

"No rabbits, or whatever you were after, and you look as if you've fallen over into the bargain. It's fairly solid and a bit slippery over the fields today."

"I didn't come over the field," he lied. "I came up the lane intending to go through the wood for pigeon. I just slipped over the ditch outside to see if there was anything about on the way." He put his considerable strength behind the next effort and the obstruction moved. Thank God! Now he would get out as quickly and politely as he could – but where would he go to keep out of the way of anyone else who happened along?

"Thanks, Peter," said Trixie sighing with relief. "You have no idea how long I've been struggling to get the thing free. This is just the sort of problem…"

"Yes, yes," said Peter impatiently. He was on the brink of finally losing control and just wanted to get away. "I must be going, I've been gone too long as it is," and, straightening his big frame, he made determinedly for the door.

But Trixie was delighted with some unexpected company over what had been for her, a dreary Christmas. "Oh, the least I can do is to get you a cup of tea, something warm inside you before you have to go out again," and before he had breath to reply she had skipped into the kitchen. "It's OK, I do have an electric kettle. We needn't wait for the hob to heat. I'm having one anyway before I take Tolly out for a turn in the trap."

Peter stopped dead. All of a sudden this whole terrible day might start to be turned round. If he kept his head, this bizarre interlude with Trixie and her fire might go some way

146

to help him out of what he was beginning to think was an impossible situation. He followed her into the kitchen, and assuming a lightness of tone which he was far from feeling asked, "Where were you thinking of going with that outfit of yours?"

"Anywhere really. Yesterday was bright, like today, so I went along the main road as far as Ardleigh and pushed a note through the blacksmith's door to ask if he could shoe Tolly next week. It got me out, but there were very few people about; all indoors with their families I expect, even the children. Taking that trap out is something I enjoy so much, though, and Tolly is a great little pony; George did me proud when he found him."

He let her chat, nodding absently as the kettle boiled. Here was some means of getting away from the immediate neighbourhood much more easily than he had first envisaged, just so long as he kept calm and hung on to his patience. He must. The thought of prison – or even, God forbid, hanging – drove him now. How far did things go before they hanged you these days? He managed a brief smile as she handed him a hot mug of tea and, lowering his head to hide his expression as he bent to sip said, "Have you been as far as Manningtree yet? I have some relatives there. It'd be a nice little ride this afternoon and a good stretch for Tolly by the estuary where all the swans gather."

Said now, and his best effort. Exhaustion was creeping through the long, unbelievable day. He looked down at his hands, now held loosely between his knees, waiting for the axe to fall.

Trixie put her cup slowly down on the table and gave the top of his head a keen look. "You sound as if you'd like to come with me," she uttered with surprise. "I thought you had to get going back to Sally." She wondered fleetingly at his motives, remembering the last time she had offered him a cup of tea. . .

Rallying, he brought her back with, "Sally isn't at home, she's visiting, that's why I went shooting. I had time on my

147

hands," hands that were beginning to shake with tired nervousness and putting down the cup, now rattling on the saucer, he gently clenched them, keeping control, waiting.

"Peter, would you like to take a Boxing Day ride in the trap to Manningtree?" she asked him formally and would have started to laugh if she had not seen his tired face almost crumble as he let out a breath. What on earth was the matter with the man? He looked ill. He certainly looked as if he needed the break of a longer holiday than the Christmas one. The final rush before he closed the bakery for the Christmas break must have washed him out. A spin out in the trap would do him good, she thought.

Later, with Tolly trotting smartly and Peter at last on his way to catch the first train he could from the railway station, he was grateful for a glimmer of respite in like he'd felt for what seemed like days. There was no one about to see them going past together; some little thing working for him for a change, till Trixie said, musingly, "I wonder what one or two of them would make of this if they saw you and me on a jaunt together?" He was suddenly jolted to be reminded that she thought it was a simple 'airing' for them both; a little holiday trip. He looked across the seat at her as she continued, "Don't worry, I've been at the receiving end of quite a bit of gossip these past four years, from what I wear to how I conduct myself on my own. I'm minding my own business, but some of them are so hidebound they think it unseemly of me to get on and do the job that two of them usually do. When I tried to build a life for myself on my own when Walter went, I must have fallen out of my pigeonhole," and she chuckled and called to Tolly, "Isn't that a fact?" and back to Peter, "You've heard the tale of the old man, the boy and the donkey, haven't you?"

He must hang on to a sense of normality by making low key answers while willing the journey to be over so that he could get away from this place. With a swooping sensation in the pit of his stomach, he started to face the thought that he

148

was actually a wanted man. He groped for the side of the trap to steady himself while a spasm of weak dizziness subsided. If someone had told him an hour ago that he could actually sit where he was, answering casual remarks, seeming so casual himself, while his world unravelled, he would never have believed it. Would she ever stop prattling?

And then, just as they'd begun to emerge to take a right turn onto the main road, George hailed them, creaking along on his old bicycle on his way up the lane to tend to his two great charges.

Trixie, very happy, as always, to see him, drew Tolly to a stop and called, "How are you George? Had a happy Christmas?"

He eyed Tolly and the trap with a horseman's scrutiny and said, "He looks well! That pony'll live on nothing, so don't you go overfeeding him, mind. Had a good dinner and rest yesterday – Tom helped out again – but glad to get back a-doin'." Then, agitatedly, he swung off the bike. "But someone's gone and shot old Jim Macaulay!"

Both turned to stare at Peter as he let out a gasp and turned white in the face. "Shot him?" echoed Trixie disbelievingly. "How on earth... When, what's happened to him?"

"No end of a carry on at Bella and Tom's. He seems in a bad way. Lost a lot of blood, he did," replied George, looking closely at Peter. "Hope he doesn't go and die. They reckon some young hooligan took his father's gun or something, and started shooting at anything that moved. Old Jim Macaulay was out walking that dog of his and it caught him in the shoulder. He was off in the ambulance to hospital when I came by just now."

Quickly, adrenalin rushing, Peter said, "I was out just now down the lane on the way to the wood to shoot, but I never saw or heard anything." His relief to hear that Macaulay was alive, that he was not wanted for murder, almost made him garrulous, and yet, he might still die. His mind slowed. He must check himself in time, before he said

149

too much. His colour had now changed from white to deep red. He'd had no alternative but to leave his shotgun 'accidentally' at Trixie's. He hoped to be well away before she had to hand it in to the police.

Tolly started to fidget in the shafts as he cooled down, wanting to get going. He liked an outing as much as any of them. "We're off on a jaunt, George, Peter wanted a lift to see his family in Manningtree and you can see Tolly wanted the exercise, so we'd better get along. I'll see you soon – poor old Macaulay!" and she turned the trap while George watched her go, pleased he'd been instrumental in fixing her up with that good little grey pony.

Peter jumped down from the trap in the High Street in Manningtree and watched Trixie go. He'd told her he didn't know how long he'd be on his visit but would walk back home across the fields if he couldn't borrow a bicycle from his family. He hung about in the street until Trixie was out of sight, before making off to the small railway station to wait for the next train. He did not care, by now, whether it went to London or the other way to Harwich, but just so long as it took him far enough away from the immediate trouble to gather what was left of his wits.

Chapter 33

The only afternoon train loudly sighed and huffed at the platform, letting off steam before its next effort. When he reached into his pocket to extract exactly the right amount of money he found, to his dismay, that he only had a copper or two. When he'd left home in such a lather, throwing on his jacket (this morning? – it seemed ages ago), patting his pockets for cash was the last thing on his mind. He'd planned to find the correct amount, pass it across the desk while keeping his head low, then slide through to the platform with the minimum of fuss. Slipping past unnoticed, without a ticket, was out of the question. There were very few passengers taking advantage of the Boxing Day service to visit relatives. He, and the direction he was taking, would easily be remembered by the railway man in the ticket office should he be asked by the police.

Cursing his bad luck, he backed away from the office before anyone there saw him, and mindlessly started walking along the valley bottom beside the river through fields of cattle grazing on the lowland grass. Anywhere would have done, just to get away from the notice of the Station staff, but he knew if he followed the river, he would eventually reach Dedham. There, he would be sufficiently far away from his home ground to keep out of sight. Big as he was, with a stamina built up over the years of heaving sacks of flour and all the heavy jobs that long hours in a bakery required, he was nevertheless nearly at the end of his strength. Only the thought of being caught and having to pay for a crime for which he still felt a sneaking justification, kept him moving doggedly on. This way, perhaps he would find a barn with hay, to rest and try to keep warm while he plotted his next move. He had to find somewhere before the waning day finally closed in and the fields and fences became too difficult to negotiate in the dark.

Head down, he plodded on into an oncoming wind which became colder and ever more cutting. His mind, after all the day's events, was now numbed to all but finding somewhere safe. It would be a consolation just to sit down and take off his boots. Dispiritedly, he raised his head to hurdle the next low gate and saw, on the skyline, a large barn out of which spilled broken bales of last year's hay. He dodged back and walked stealthily along the screening hedge until he was opposite the barn. There were lights on in the farmhouse windows further back, but no one was in the yard. On an evening like this, anyone with any sense would be glad to be indoors around the fire.

He could hardly register in his mind that just forty-eight hours ago, he had had a 'normal' life, albeit a troubled one. Now, with the extraordinary events of this day, he'd put himself beyond normality and basic comforts. He could hardly believe it.

He paused to look and listen. There were no dogs in the yard – no barking. Gathering himself, he leapt the fence and made quickly for the sanctuary of the barn. He had often felt alone during his time in the army but at least there was food at the end of the day, even if he had to cook it. For now, he was too tired and miserable to care for anything else but to curl up in a corner, get as comfortable as he could, and sleep.

He awoke stiff with cold well before the late first light dawned and was forced to scramble to his feet and move some blood through his limbs. He easily found a tap in the yard for a mouthful or two of water but, hungry though he was, food would have to wait. For now, he had to be well away from the barn before anyone saw him, so he made his way back to the river valley where his steps had first led him, no further inspired with a definite plan this morning than he had been yesterday. Now, though, in the back of his mind was a growing thankfulness that he had not gone out of the area completely. At least this way he might have a chance to find out how bloody old Macaulay was recovering… or not, and act accordingly. Leaving the one place he'd known all his life to try to make a fresh start in an area foreign to him would add to his burdens, so far as he could see. He'd have to take his chances here.

As he walked, the sky lightened. High up, a dozen swans, glowing white against the moody cloud cover, wings singing, made to land in the wide, salty estuary, well beyond the path he was taking. The busy movement of the water capped the surface with white, swept plumes. Peter strode along the river bank, oblivious to all but the idea of somehow finding food and more suitable shelter for the night. Getting warmer now, but still sharp set with unaccustomed hunger, he walked for an hour or two before he came to a tributary, a small, deep cut diverted from the main flow. Irritated, he started to circle round this branch of water hoping to find a crossing to take him back to the river bank itself.

Inland further, rounding a bend in this small tributary, he suddenly came upon a group of buildings in front of which sat a middle-aged man painting a punt which was upside down on the bank. There were another two dozen or so punts and rowing boats lying haphazardly around and in a nearby lean-to was a stack of old cushions and a few frayed oars. Everything, including the two railway carriages bordering this outpost, was washed in a dismal uniform grey under the lowering gloom of the morning. It was too late to back-track and Peter made to wish the man a formal good morning and pass by.

"You found me then," said the man, sitting back on his haunches and resting the brush on the tin of paint. Peter almost looked behind him, startled, to see who the man was speaking to, when he resumed. "They said in the village you'd been asking about a job. Well, I could do with a bit of help here, as I told them. It's always the same this time of year, getting ready for the summer."

Peter's mouth opened and closed, opened again, "Um,

what is the job?" Another try, "What do you want doing, then?" He could see the possibilities as he spoke. The man had already seen him anyway. He was on a backwater he never knew existed, so there was an excellent chance he was unlikely to meet anyone who would give him away.

"Can you paint?" the man's words cut across his thoughts.

"Well, yes. Yes," was the best Peter could manage.

"We'll see how you go then, but I shan't be paying you much. They said you were passing through, anyway, so nothing permanent." And with that, the man simply passed the pot and brush over to Peter and got up, his hands dusting down his oily, dark trousers as if it would make any difference to them. He walked off into the first railway carriage where, judging by the table and chair Peter could see as he opened the door, the man probably lived. Clumsily, Peter picked up the brush, slippery as a fish in his big hands, dipped it into the dark grey paint and diffidently began to apply it to the hull.

The man came out again with two mugs of something steaming and presented him with one of the teas. "I bet you're another of them from the Army in Colchester," he guessed. "There used to be a lot like you just after the end of the war – not so many now. Homeless and nowhere to go when you do get out from serving your time – in or out of the glasshouse!" He seemed to find this very funny and gave a choked laugh, two yellow teeth revealed in a long, thin mouth.

Peter had no idea who the poor devil was whose place he seemed to be taking, but considered the other old soldier might be well out of it if he travelled on. For the time being, at least, he had better stay here as the proprietor of this run-down boating establishment evidently counted on his doing.

He painted all day, grateful for the corned beef sandwich wedge at midday from his boss whom he called Mr Partridge; no Christian name had been offered. He tucked his blistered hands up close to his sides in the dark of the second railway carriage, lying on a damp, cold mattress under a rough blanket at nightfall. In between, he had hoisted, pulled and pushed the rest of the boats into some sort of order, ready for mending, sanding and painting. He felt he could have eaten a horse, and might well have done, in the surprisingly tasty meat and vegetable stew Mr Partridge dished up when dusk called a halt to work.

Payment had not been further discussed, but Peter felt he had made progress enough, such as it was, for one day. No awkward questions had been asked. The man, Partridge, was evidently used to taking advantage of itinerant help. Peter had at least eaten fairly well and heartened, he resolved to smarten up the inside of the railway carriage and wash a few things as soon as he could. It was only too evident that there was not, nor ever had been, a Mrs Partridge, much less a covey of little Partridges.

Chapter 34

Having dropped Peter off, Trixie turned the trap before the large stone swan, set as a fountain in the middle of a round lake. This landmark had been in front of the maltings mill for as long as the villagers could remember. She walked Tolly on long, loose reins beside the run of the estuary where swans crowded the maltings outlet seeking the leavings from brewing. Gulls called plaintively, feathers ruffled, as they lifted and swung away on a rising wind. Shivering slightly, she walked Tolly up the small incline to the high street, desultory window shopping as she went, looking over the side of the trap.

Lights were going on in the few houses set back from the main street and she could see the glow of fires and some of the families within from her high perch. A woman crossed the room to adjust an ornament on her tree. These Christmas trees were a new idea from abroad and unlikely to be taken up by the hard pressed Settlement tenants, she guessed. Another, glad to be comfortably indoors with her family on this holiday evening, thrust her face close to the window to look more keenly at the lone outsider driving the little grey pony. Then she pulled her dark curtains with a decisive swish, shutting Trixie out abruptly, as if she had no business to be passing by on her own at this time of evening. They passed Doctor Beckett's surgery, the light from which cast a glow across the giant apothecary jars in the dispensary window. Trixie remembered Elsie telling her those jars, with their vibrant coloured contents, had cured many of Barry's tummy aches when he'd no more than glanced at them.

The street was quiet; no one else about. While the day waned a sullen wind had arisen along the shore. Trixie now became aware of it cutting into her face. Taking the reins in one hand, she defensively lifted the collar of her coat to hold against her.

The old empty feeling returned as memories of Walter and of Christmases which seemed so long ago, crept to the forefront of her mind. She believed, now, that she would always miss Walter.

Tolly stretched his neck low to blow softly down his nose on a relaxed rein, then picked up his stride as the wind cooled his damp skin under the wide leather straps of his harness. Trixie sat up straighter. Now she wanted to get back home before the dusk became darkness and the 'trot on' to Tolly was just what he'd been waiting for.

With one accord, she and Tolly took the trap up the steep hill and the right turn which led them both home to food and warmth. Action, and the spirit of the tough little pony shook off Trixie's brief melancholy and she talked to him as she often did. "If that cat's in my chair by the fire when I get in, he'll have to move over pretty damn quick." Tolly, now so much part of her life, like the rest of the cosseted animals in her care, loved hearing her voice and shook his head as if he doubted it.

It took time, when Trixie reached the smallholding, to take Tolly out of the traces, strap a blanket across his back and feed him. A big rack of hay would soon warm his insides. On George's sound advice, she did not feed him oats. "That pony's a good doer and don't need any of them oats, he'll live on fresh air, and work well for you," she heard him say. "Don't go letting him get laminitis or something." George well knew she'd be likely to kill Tolly with kindness, costing herself a small fortune into the bargain, if he didn't watch her and scare her off it.

She walked round the piggery, two sows now asleep and snoring deep in clean straw. She checked the goats and chickens. She'd have to get help moving the ark to a fresh site over the fallow vegetable patch soon; she was grateful that George or Benny would always help there without any fuss.

157

Thankfully, she shut the kitchen door and moved through to the living room to hold her cold hands in front of the fire. She had seen the gun propped up behind the kitchen door as she'd shut it, and guessed Peter would call in for it on his way home tomorrow. He would not have left it loaded and it was quite safe where it was. She moved to the window and drew her own curtains against the cold outside world. Inky yawned and stretched with contentment as he settled further into her chair.

———————————

The next morning, as she jerked open the sticking door with an old saucepan full of cooked, warm potato peelings for the chickens in her hand, she nearly let it go all over Sergeant Willow's smart uniform as he was about to knock. Startled, she thrust the hot saucepan out of the way. Having given her a brief "Good Morning," he asked directly, "Where did you drop Peter Starling off yesterday, Mrs Langham? George down the road has just told us you took him to Manningtree in the trap." Sergeant Willow was not one to stand on ceremony or waste time in chitchat.

"Yes, to see some relatives of his; having the day off from baking." She looked from the Sergeant to the Constable who had driven him in the big, black car parked in the lane outside her gate. "I set him down by the swan near the mill – why, what's happened to him?"

The Constable, who knew most of the tenants well, looked away and up the garden. The Sergeant ignored the question but said, "He told George he'd been out shooting in the morning when you both met George down the lane, didn't he?"

"Oh, yes!" light dawning, "I have his gun here where he left it behind the door. I expected him to pick it up today. He must have stayed overnight in Manningtree."

"We'll take it with us for now," said Sergeant Willow, decisively and Trixie quietly turned about to collect the gun, then thoughtfully handed it over.

"Is he all right, Sergeant?" she asked.

More forthcoming now he had the shotgun in his possession, Sergeant Willow said, "There's been an unexplained shooting and a Mr Macaulay has been hurt. All firearms in the district must be accounted for. Lucky you had Mr Starling's, it saves me calling there again. Do you happen to have the address of the people he was visiting yesterday?"

"Sally will know, if you do call back," Trixie said and was surprised when the Sergeant replied, "We've just been there – no sign of Mrs Starling either." He turned on his heel to leave before Trixie asked any more questions, the Constable trotting after him, trying to manoeuvre in front of him in time to open the back door for the Sergeant. Trixie went indoors, disquieted, but with another Christmas safely over at last, she thankfully picked up where she left off, taking the cooled potato peelings to mix with the chicken mash, grateful that it was just a routine day for her, as she began the round of necessary tasks.

Chapter 35

Sergeant Willow threw down his pen in disgust and leaned back in his chair. "I give up! Some cock and bull story fed me as if I was an imbecile about those two walking together, then Starling trips up and the gunshot clips Macaulay's shoulder. An accident? I don't think so!"

Constable Paul lowered the table barrier across his desk and came through from the front office. He'd heard one side of the story when the Sergeant was on the telephone a moment ago.

"That man Macaulay won't make a charge, and I know why! What a bloody mess. We go hiking round houses pulling in all the firearms in the district, Starling disappears off the face of the earth, old Macaulay looks me straight in the eye and gives me this!"

"How about a brew Sarg?" asked Constable Paul, helpless in the face of this onslaught. That did it! Sergeant Willow needed action, not cups of tea. He banged down in his chair, smacked his hands on the table and stood up grabbing his hat as he gave Constable Paul a sour look, and stopped just short of slamming the door on his way out.

Constable Paul shook his head. The Sergeant hadn't been the same since old Macaulay had refused to co-operate in charges being brought for Peter Starling's arrest. Nothing frustrated him more than watching a felon getting away with it, obstructing the course of justice while the Sergeant's hands were tied. And where was the felon, Paul wondered. All enquiries at the railway station in Manningtree had yielded nothing. No one had seen a trace, nor heard a whisper. All seemed to have been indoors, and rightly so, on that cold, windy Boxing Day. As a rule, nothing like this ever occurred

160

in his neighbourhood, nothing to get the police teeth into and the Sergeant was affability itself – well, sometimes, anyway.

Now, here was Macaulay running off with Starling's wife. It was all too clear that Starling had taken his shotgun and followed Macaulay. Constable Paul even wondered if he himself would be above wanting to shove a shotgun up a wife-poacher's behind to help him on his way if he tried it on with his wife. But to go as far as to pull the trigger, and this was so obviously the way it had happened. Starling must have been in a ferment of despair. He could have killed old Macaulay and been had up and hanged. Lucky for him that Macaulay's shoulder was mending and Jim Macaulay was home and wanted to lay the matter to rest. He was just trying to cope with running his pub again.

Chapter 36

In the dismal month Peter had been working for Mr Partridge renovating the wooden boats, each man continued to be reticent with the other. Partridge had employed too many casual helpers. It didn't do to enquire at all closely into their lives. On Peter's side was relief that his boss believed he was a refugee from the Army. He was careful not to let the truth slip out in an unguarded moment.

Partridge was glad to lean on Peter's strength to manhandle the boats which were getting heavier for him every year, and Peter was glad of the respite and the accommodation, such as it was, better now he had painted and freshened the inside of his railway carriage. In fact, it was a novelty to him to improve his own living space and, in spite of the general January damp alongside the tributary, he was able to drag out the mattress on one or two windy days to air and dry.

At the end of the first week, Partridge had presented Peter with two crumpled one pound notes for his work and with bed and board thrown haphazardly in, Peter felt his situation could be worse, though he thought longingly of his bakery and wondered what was going on above this valley. Just how bad was the mess he was in? Had Macaulay died? In an effort to find out, he had ventured cautiously into the main street once or twice, past the water mill and round the corner of The Marlborough to read the headlines in the general shop which sold papers. Nothing. Surely if there had been a murder in the county there would be almost daily mention in the national as well as the local press. It would be far too close to home to discuss such a matter with Partridge without exacerbating any suspicions he might have about Peter's reasons. Ex-Army man with a family life destroyed by war or desertion was one thing, shooting a man (maybe killing him) was another.

Peter sat in the yard waiting for the kettle to boil over a wood fire he'd made with the waste from the boats he'd been mending. There was a discreet splash from the river bank. A water vole sent ripples back to him as it swam straight and fast across to the other side. He reflected on his backwoods life now and contrasted it with the secure, clean environment he had forfeited by his lawless action and hot-headedness. He looked down at the tear across one knee of his trousers – his one pair of trousers – and considered that he must, sooner or later, venture into a shop to make one or two purchases of new clothes. He certainly could not ask Partridge to do that for him. He did not need to venture dangerously out to buy food; Partridge did that while Peter carried on doing the heavy work.

He had to admit to a growing restlessness, hardly controlled, to find out what was happening to Sally and the bakery but, warring with this anxiety was the knowledge that he could not afford to be seen by anyone who might recognise him. Fear of imprisonment was overriding. For now, the dark days were accentuated by hours of rain, as if it was not damp and uncomfortable enough on the banks of the tributary inlet and an ennui born of winter gloom and despondency bore down on him.

One morning, a particularly high tide almost breached the bank on which the two men were working under scant cover in the rain, enough to make Partridge pause and take stock. He recommended that they move the remaining mended and painted boats a little higher. They were more than thankful that night to retire to their respective living quarters away from the evening's driving rain and oncoming darkness, in the hope of better weather in the morning.

When Peter awoke it was to find water swirling under the wheels of the railway carriages, and the mended boats, which they had stacked in tidy rows under cover, were floating, or half submerged in the water in chaotic disarray, while the water in the little tributary crept dangerously up the slope from its breached bank.

Bewildered, Peter waded over to Partridge's carriage and up the steps to thump on his door. "Tide's over the bank man, look!" and he waved an arm across the width of their camp.

"Good God! What's happened?" This from Partridge as he pulled on his boots and charged down the steps behind Peter. Water impeded their progress in working their way to where the bank should have been. Aghast, both men stood looking from left to right on the brink of the deep water cut, trying to make sense of it all.

"This is crazy, Peter. We'll have to grab what boats we can that haven't already floated away," but Partridge still stood dumbfounded trying to decide where to start.

Peter waded in to grasp the first boat banging against another, their mooring lines fortunately tangled, which kept them near the submersed bank. Both men worked hard all morning to salvage boats and equipment, soaked to the skin, wading into the swollen cut. Working as a team, they drove the boats which were loose and floating here and there and upside down, to a safer shore, tying them to anything which would hold them fast. Partridge swore nothing like it had ever happened before in all the years he'd been there. He couldn't understand it. Mercifully, the main rage of the flood had spent itself by the time it had reached this backwater and at least the railway carriages were spared. Only the wheels remained submerged until the spate subsided.

Exhausted, Peter stumbled up the steps into his temporary home, which looked more welcoming to him now than at any time before. Water ran down in rivulets as he peeled off his drenched coat inside the door and let it drop to the floor. His feet, sodden in thick socks, oozed across the cracked lino as he found his way to the tiny toilet area and reached at last for a towel. Both men had now done all they could to rescue the boats and he and Partridge, nearly at a standstill, had retreated too tired to speak, to their respective living quarters.

A daunting sight met them in the morning. Though they had salvaged the majority of the boats, wood from others, which had smashed against trees in fields far from the normal flow of the river, had been washed against the railway carriages. Debris still plunged through the never ending water. Peter watched from the door of the carriage as swirling water hurled anything in its path onto submerged obstructions which, only days ago, were landmarks familiar to them. For the first time, Peter actually felt sorry for poor old Partridge. His small business, shabby as it was, would take a long while to recover.

It took a day or two to filter through to their little backwater that an abnormally high spring tide had combined with low pressure and flooded the whole of the east coast. Across from Partridge and Peter, on the main part of the river, a smarter boating establishment had lost almost all of their boats, which floated off in the dangerous waters and the teashop on the shore nearby had been entirely swept away in the heavy current. As the enormity of the disaster penetrated to them, they were comforted that their tributary hadn't suffered more. They were thankful that their ground was higher and the damage that might have been was so much less.

As it was, the immediate dangers concentrated Peter's mind and took it momentarily off his other worries. He and his boss took turns anxiously to watch the state of the tidal backwater for days after the huge flood. If it did nothing else, at least, thought Peter, it made him appreciate a roof over his head; that hadn't been lost. Neither were most of the boats he had been working on these past weeks.

A day or two after that dreadful morning, Partridge knocked on Peter's door to share a whisky with him in acknowledgement of Peter's enormous effort. It was a celebration of their survival of a national disaster.

From that day, an uneasy friendship began to develop between the tight-lipped Peter and the taciturn Mr Partridge.

February melded into March as together they set to rights the damage the surging tide had done to their camping area and gradually Partridge replaced the sundry domestic and work items lost in the fray. A spirit of pulling together did much to enhance their tentative understanding of each other, but both also knew that one day Peter would have to leave; Partridge knew they always did, particularly an edgy young man like this one, and Peter knew that there would come a time soon when he simply could no longer live without knowing what had happened to Sally and bloody old Macaulay. And lastly, what about the bakery going to rack and ruin? He would have to take the risk of being seen by someone who knew him in an effort to find out where he stood.

Chapter 37

Time was going on and Peter still could not be found. Jim moved back to the pub and Sally was seen there a lot "helping him in the bar until his arm heals properly", she said. This unseemly arrangement was cause for gossip, mainly among the women, and the words 'brazen hussy' came into conversation more than once when Sally's defection was being discussed. The Wooden Fender was a lot quieter, with less custom than before, but Peter and Sally chose to ignore that worry. They could only wait for the furore to die down and hope for customers to trickle back when something else caught their interest. They had no alternative but to weather it.

One or two of the wives disapproved of what they saw as suspiciously indecent circumstances at the Wooden Fender sufficiently to attempt to deter their husbands from calling in for a pint. Mrs Morgan was in the forefront of the condemnation.

"A barmaid, and that's all she's good for," shrilled Annie to Fred who had been edging to the door to take his cap off the hook.

"Well, I only want a pint," replied Fred in a rare turn of spirit, "not the bloody barmaid!" He stood, cap in hand, looking all injured innocence. "I thought you women were always too busy to gossip about a poor young girl like that." He fled as his wife came across the room with a finger wagging in front of her. It had got him out of the house anyway, even if he had been chased out by his own missus. He clapped his cap on the side of his head and stepped up the road with lively intent. Getting back in again would be a bit more difficult! "Meet trouble when it comes," he muttered grandly, buoyed up by the thought of a pint.

Annie put her views across the fence to Bella when she saw her hanging the washing out next day.

"Fancy that girl leaving a man like Peter and living over the brush with that old Macaulay," she said in high indignation.

Bella, immediately defensive for Jean and Sally whom she'd known all her young life answered, "Oh is she, Annie? How do you know?"

"Well, it's obvious, isn't it? There she is, no home to go to and there at that pub all the time."

Bella always held that she hadn't time for gossip, not like some of the women on the Settlement. There was more than a hint of superiority in this, as near snobbery as Bella would ever get. When it came to defending her few good friends who had been neighbours for years, she was a small, round force to contend with and a quick, sharp tongue in reply.

"Do you think for one moment, Annie, that Sally wanted to cause her husband grief?" Surely you must realise there must have been a good reason for her to leave Peter. I always say, you have to live a marriage to know it!"

This hit home with more meaning than Bella intended. She had often heard through the kitchen wall the raised voices of Annie and Fred. This was usually when Fred had returned from the Wooden Fender and started 'speaking out of turn', as Annie put it, but Bella would never have hinted that she had heard. Annie had an uncomfortable inkling that Bella might be getting at her. What with Fred going off like that yesterday and Bella being stand-offish as usual, she wished she'd never started this conversation. "Just what do you mean by that, Bella Whitley?"

Quickly Bella realised where this was leading and countered with, "Oh, Annie, I really don't understand what's going on there, but it would take a lot for the women in our day to leave our husbands, wouldn't it?"

Mollified, Annie metaphorically gathered up her skirts and, disappointed in the way it had all gone, no newsy gossip

– no details at all – turned on her heel and went indoors. Later Bella heard her clattering buckets while emptying her washing out of the sink, then taking her frustration out on the mangle. Annie was fed up with Bella sometimes. It was what came from living next door on top of each other.

But Bella felt very uncertain of her stand on the problems of Peter and Sally, despite her strong words. Knowing them both, she could not conceive of a situation between those two which might have led Sally to actually leave her husband and live openly with that man Macaulay. Jean had never hinted of any serious discord between them – but, of course, she wouldn't - good friends though they were, it wouldn't have done.

What on earth had made the girl leave Peter in this way? They had seemed so happy together at the start, and Sally had been given so much to be thankful for. It just wouldn't have happened when Bella was young.

But the day hadn't yet finished with Bella, for later, as Bella and Tom lay comfortably warm, side by side in their big bed, the unmistakable tickle of a flea started along Bella's leg, then sprang to Tom's side. Both of them slid out of bed in the well-rehearsed way and, found themselves actually whispering to each other so as not to alarm the flea. Bella shot off to find the bar of soap kept near the ewer and dipped it quickly into the glass of water on the little table beside the bed. With one accord, they whisked back the bedclothes and Bella pounced on the bed, her bottom in the air, with the soap fast in her hand, ready to smack down on the flea. Tom, always slower, stood back and watched her, stifling a laugh. She had time to shoot him one of her infamous glares before renewing the attack over the folded back bedclothes. Involuntarily jumping in time with the flea, she broke the rhythm with a smart aim, pinning the flea to the soap. Triumphantly, she raised the soap. Then, deftly picking off the flea, she dunked it in the glass of water.

"That's another one this week!" a baffled Tom exclaimed.

169

"I know where they come from too," Bella said, unhappily. "Along the pipes in our airing cupboard. There must be a way through from Annie's, but I can't find it. I've spoken to Annie about it before but she seems to take them as a fact of life. You know her, she doesn't seem to get upset about such things. Says, 'Well, fleas are clean enough, not as bad as some insects, and there's only one or two. You can catch 'em with a bit of soap, gal', then she goes off to sing hymns."

She looked very indignant as Tom came close and held her. "I'll have a word with Fred. Perhaps he can talk some sense to her. I'll also have a look in that cupboard and see if I can block where they're coming in."

"It would just have to happen again today when I've already had words with Annie, Tom." Bella, now thoroughly awake, would take a while to settle down.

Bella and Annie, diverse in their characters, were also vastly different in their attitudes towards keeping their homes comfortable. While dust, and worse, to Annie meant a home well-lived in, to Bella it meant neglect and disregard. It was bound to jar now and again, but it was essential to their peace of mind, that they continue to go a long way to settle their differences.

Chapter 38

Sally worried quietly as to how Peter was and where he was living. She fervently hoped one day he would forgive her and be happy himself.

There was nothing she wanted at the bakery, but not so long ago she had called in on Mr Timothy, the solicitor, to prepare a six month lease for a couple who had answered her advertisement to take over the bakery for the time being. If ever Peter turned up again, and he might if he ever learned that Jim did not want to press charges for the shooting, she could at least hand him over the money from the bakery rent.

Jim and Sally were pleasant and welcoming to all who called into the Wooden Fender and gradually the customers became used to seeing Sally behind the bar. Although she and Jim wanted to marry, they had to be content to live with each other until Peter turned up or sent word. Sally might then persuade him to give her a divorce. When it became generally known that Peter had actually shot Jim and that Jim would not seek redress and wanted to forget the incident, conversely it helped their customers and neighbours accept their situation with more sympathy. "So that's what they mean when they talk about an ill wind," said Jim.

For now, they were both happy to be together just living quietly from day to day – until they were forced to announce to Jean and Bob, at least, that there was a baby on the way. Thrilled that at last she would have a much dreamed of baby, Sally nevertheless checked her headlong rush to confide in Jean. Ever since she had taken off on this life with Jim, there had been a reserve that was almost shy between her and her mother which stilled her first intention to sweep Jean along in a blithe momentum. Sally was already overwhelmed with a sense of fierce protection of the coming child and, having worn to forgiveness much of the scorn which had faced her and Jim at the beginning, she felt confident to ride out any new wave of criticism. Jim, delighted at such happy and unexpected news of a baby, watched Sally closely with ready support, knowing that soon it would be noticed and set tongues wagging once more. Sally couldn't go on working behind the bar for much longer.

Now it was March; they could take time off during the day and walk across the open fields in the strengthening sunshine. They watched the hare slant across in front of them in the blustery Essex winds – sometimes a dozen or more would be skirmishing at once, raised on hind legs in boxing stance. The skies were vast and seemingly low over the great, flat lands alive with skylarks' song. Shadows moved over the fields, while the wind lifted and flattened a sea of young corn.

It was an enchanting time for Sally, who suddenly found herself intensely interested in the outdoor changes of an advancing spring. From a life focussed indoors, working daily at the bakery, her world had gently widened, first with Jim and now awaiting the baby's birth. Simple walks and small pleasures were balm after the recent storm they had just come through and this happy calm did most to heal and strengthen them. These walks were getting shorter for Sally as she got heavier than, she said, a pregnant woman had any right to be, with obvious delight. Jim told her the truth – she glowed; mysteriously, he said. And with her slowly revealing secret her happiness was catching. Although they both looked forward so much to summer and the baby's birth, they were content for now to wait and coast along while their world settled down.

Sweet rationing had ended at last and Jim bought Sally a large box of chocolates to celebrate. "I feel big enough now," she told him looking down at her bump in disbelief. "Do you think its twins?"

He laughed, "I would not want you a scrap different from the way you're going along now," he answered. Then, serious, "You do know how much I love you, don't you, Sally." He said it as a statement.

She answered no more than a simple "Yes". She understood that he had given her these words as a gift and did not need to be told now how much she loved him in return.

Chapter 39

By May-time Benny the postman had become fed up with everyone on his rounds asking if he'd heard anything of Peter's whereabouts. All the gossip these days seemed to be about Peter and those two at the pub.

Once more, he'd narrowly missed being drenched with the contents of Granny Cafferty's night-time pot. She'd thrown it, as usual, across the path onto a patch of rhubarb in the garden from the shelter of the door, to save her stepping outside in her bare feet. He knew she'd catch him one day, daft old bat. Was it any wonder her daughter allowed a large white chicken in and out of the house to pick up the crumbs from under their table, and sometimes on top of it? Hygiene wasn't a top priority for some folk he called on. He saw a good deal of life, good and bad on his round. It was a matter of ordinary pride for most women to keep a clean home in difficult circumstances. These rural houses were still very basic and few women put on much weight as they tore around from one physically demanding job to another.

Jean, Bob's wife, was always working hard scrubbing floors and cleaning windows and doing all the big and little jobs of just keeping a home ticking over. Benny admired a woman like Jean. She even managed to keep their huge flower garden tidy and the lawn mowed, while Bob concentrated on the vegetables and a large rectangle of raspberry canes from which, in season, Jean made fruit pies and jam to give to any little show or function. He remembered then, with amusement, that he had heard that Mrs Morgan had cheated at the last autumn do, and she a pillar of the Sunday School! He grinned. It seemed that the Girl Guide leader, who did not live on the Settlement, was asked to judge at the autumn fete. She had been heard to remark to Mrs Jarvis that she detected Rowntrees Strawberry Jelly in Mrs Morgan's jam. He found it hard to see how anyone would want to win a jam competition that much.

Stopping now by Jean's home, he propped his bicycle up at the top of the steps leading down to the garden gate. He found Jean in the garden, her arms encased in a pair of Bob's heavy gauntlets struggling with a length of determined briar. She was trying to tie it back down to the fine link fence where the single pink dog rose flowers blew in the breeze, drifting petals. A rope of roses dotted along the wire in glorious disarray before it slid behind the buddleia. Peacock and tortoiseshell butterflies lifted and alighted on the long purple blooms as she worked. Not for the first time did Benny think of her as an ideal woman, dressed today in what she would call her gardening dress, blue and close-fitting, her house overall being discarded, for once.

She gave him a big smile and stepped back from the thorny roses but was not quick enough to avoid a briar stem lashing back and catching her arm as her loosely-tied string came undone. She grasped her arm as she looked down quickly to the dark blob of blood oozing from the puncture, her smile fading to a slight frown. She would never know, if he could help it, how attractive he found her and how much he wanted to take her arm – so tenderly – and… He'd be the wrong end of those gauntlets and lose his job into the bargain if he didn't pull himself together. He had no doubt of this woman's ability to see off unwelcome attention, but the unattainable woman was always so appealing. Jean, completely unaware of his daydreaming, distractedly rubbed her arm, before reaching for the two letters Benny held wondering why the man always seemed to be in a gormless trance. How he ever delivered the right letter to anyone, going around the way he did, was a mystery to her.

Benny, who had always felt guilty in his hopeless longings for Jean, guarded himself from moving to cradle her arm – and his tongue from comment – except to say lamely,

175

"You look busy, Jean. Two letters today!"

"I want to get ahead with the work in the garden while I can, Benny. I need to be free and on hand when the grandchild is born. I'm even tying the roses in granny-knots now, I'm so looking forward to it."

On safe ground now, Benny said, "I saw Sally this morning and told her I had two letters for you. She sends her love and says she's feeling very well. She knew you'd ask me how she was"

"Thanks, Benny. Fancy I'm going to be a grandmother – and Bob a granddad! That's something to think about," she laughed, and took the letters indoors as he turned to go.

She must be feeling very relieved, he thought, that that girl of hers is settled at last. Bit of a scandal but can't be helped. She can't get married if she can't get divorced first, but in all the years Benny had known Sally he thought she had never looked happier. And that baby will want for nothing, he guessed. He would never know just how much anguish Jean and Bob had suffered as they'd tried to understand the actions of their wayward daughter. Just as it seemed that Sally had almost weathered the scandal of living with Jim, they now faced the inevitable disparaging remarks whispered by some of the neighbours when they heard of the illegitimate baby on the way.

Benny picked his bicycle up from the top of the steps and went across the road to Bella and Tom's house. He called her formally 'Mrs Whitley', not even 'Elizabeth' and would never dream of calling her Tom's pet name – it wouldn't do; she could be very cutting for a round rather comfortable looking little person, he had found. It was knowing all his customers and touching on the periphery of their lives all these years which made his job so interesting. He could not imagine doing his job anywhere else. Being 'posted' himself!

Chapter 40

Well after the long weeks it had taken to reinstate the boats and equipment following the great floods, Partridge came back from the main street and found Peter weighing a large stone in his hand, preparing to throw. A huge brown rat had become so tame round their site that it was, at that moment, sitting up and washing its whiskers near a gap in the hedge. They both stood there outraged, Peter wishing, for the first time since he'd shot Macaulay, that he still had his gun.

"You must be bored about here all the time boy," said Partridge. "I've just passed one of the cottages up top and there's a bike advertised. Two pounds it'll cost you. Dear, but they don't come cheap these days. There's not many bikes about that people will part with. It'll take you down a few lanes and about a bit. What do you think?"

"Damn good idea. Which cottage is it?" Much as the idea appealed, Peter felt uncertain. He was reluctant to venture into the main street, much less knock on a door.

Old Partridge recognised his dilemma. "You make yourself useful here and get a bite to eat together, I'll nip back and find out about it. If I think it's any good, then I'll get it. OK?"

"Yes – and thanks," said Peter. It would take some of the mind-numbing boredom off. Anything would.

When Partridge came back he was wheeling the bicycle and wearing a wide grin which showed all his teeth. Peter would never get used to this disconcerting exposure of Partridge's false teeth. He was only thankful that this very white, even line was shown so rarely. Partridge stored them, wrapped in a red scarf, in a chest in his bedroom, using them only for special occasions. He was always afraid they might break in two. But there was no need to waste his best smile day-to-day on Peter, and Peter had become comfortable with the two off-white hopefuls still doing duty for the whole set. This morning, however, he'd deemed the occasion of bargaining for a bicycle warranted the charm of a full grin. He never realised the wolfish effect it had.

"Got it for one pound ten shillings," he said happily, and proffered the remaining ten shilling note, this time not screwed and crumpled as if he wanted to remember every part of it before he had to give it up. Peter had risen in his esteem since his stalwart rescue of most of his boats during the flood. "There, that'll put us right. Come Friday when your pay is due, you'll already have had it. (Peter didn't need to be reminded that Partridge would not forget and pay him twice).

"See how you get on with the old bike," Partridge added, full of glee at his hard bargaining.

Now Peter had the means to get about more easily, an uncontained impatience took hold of him to go back home and find out what was going on. Later that day he wheeled out the bicycle and set off. He took a good hour to find his way, just before dusk, up out of the valley and along the roads to the lane nearest his bakery. He dropped the bicycle half into a ditch along the field beyond and crept along the hedge to the back of the bakehouse. There was a light on inside and the heady smell of baking bread wafted from the building, nostalgic and appetising. He prowled, rage burning his mind. How dare someone just walk in and carry on without a by your leave? But he had paid for his hot-headedness already. It had got him just where he was now, on the outside looking in. He would not make the same mistake again.

Taking a deep breath, he moved cautiously round to the front of the building and saw a To Let sign, lying on its side by the bakery wall. So that's what had happened! It was a relief to know this much. Sally couldn't sell the place, which still belonged to him, of course, but neither was it going to rack and ruin. He wondered once more where she was and what she was doing. She had been in the back of his mind all along. She obviously wasn't there if she'd let the place. Curtains were drawn and saved him from the decision of whether to risk a look through the window or not. The last thing he wanted was to set up was a hue and cry or to show himself in the neighbourhood.

He worked his way back to the boundary of the bakery and reluctantly lifted his eyes to the Wooden Fender across the space of the field between. Lights on there as well, of course, with the pub open and doing business. He would dearly love to throw all consideration for the consequences aside and walk in through the door to find out just what had happened but, it was out of the question. He'd done well so far but he still had to find his way safely back to the valley in the dark using the dim headlight that had come with the bicycle.

Chapter 41

Mr Timothy walked into the reception area of his firm. Elsie sat at her new Remington typing a lease with great concentration. If she made a mistake on this page, she would have to take it out of the machine and start again before it could be sewn up to make the whole accurate document. Leases, typed both sides of the page, were often long-winded affairs, and she wanted to get this one safely done as soon as she could.

"Please don't be offended Mrs Armstrong but you will find that I keep a safe in my office that has private files. I tell all my ladies about this. There are always certain situations which will arise from the fact that this is such a close neighbourhood, everyone knowing everyone else. It therefore becomes expedient that certain information does not become knowledge to my staff. It helps you, in that you will not have the possible burden of knowing something about your friends which may put you in a potentially awkward position. We can all rest assured that private information will not be forthcoming from this office."

"I quite understand, Mr Timothy." He doesn't trust us, she thought, and blast, she'd made a mistake! And why did he always sound so pompous?

Mr Timothy hurried out of the office to see a client while Elsie pondered on what he'd said. She was here to type correspondence and answer the phone, to receive and, on occasions, comfort, clients while waiting for Mr Timothy to be free. During the course of all this, she would learn much about many of her neighbours. The great majority were in trouble by the time they came to Mr Timothy's and though it made her job interesting, she could see how some information which would inevitably come her way could be devastating to the people involved, should she whisper it to anyone outside the office. She well understood the need for absolute discretion without his explaining it to her. She became suddenly glad that if certain matters arose that were closer to home, she would be ignorant of them and unable to spill the details. Yes, she did understand. It was a good safeguard.

Mr Timothy took a phone call from Peter who called himself "Mr Green" and enquired if his firm had dealt with the lease to the bakery and when it might come free, whereupon he might be interested.

"I really cannot say, Mr Green. What made you think we were the solicitors dealing with the matter of this lease?"

"I phoned the estate agents on the To Let signboard who advertised it. They told me your firm dealt with it," said Peter. He'd have to work hard here to get what he wanted.

"Should the likelihood occur, Mr Green, would there be a phone number where I might reach you to inform you?"

Peter ignored the question and said "I know Mrs Starling well, but have been away for some time and lost touch. If you'd please let me know where I could contact her, perhaps we can discuss it."

It all reminded the solicitor of the peculiar situation which had arisen with the Starlings at the bakery. Mr Timothy had some sympathy with Peter Starling, still missing. He wondered if word had filtered through to the man that he was no longer wanted as a criminal. He remembered that, as Mr Macaulay would not have Peter Starling arrested, he had let the matter drop.

"I'm afraid any contact with Mrs Starling on the matter of the bakery lease must first come through this office, Mr Green. I'm sure you understand. If you give me your phone number, I could call you when I've spoken to Mrs Starling."

"I'm sorry, Mr Timothy, but I'm not on the phone. I'm calling from a phonebox. Could you call Mrs Starling and ask if she'd meet me somewhere? If it is a six month lease and the new people don't want to renew it, it may be in Mrs

Starling's interest to have another tenant in mind."

"I will most certainly contact my client and ask her if she wishes to discuss this with you, Mr Green and perhaps you would be good enough to send me your request in writing, so that I will have an address to send any relevant correspondence. I can then keep you informed." Mr Timothy heard a sigh of relief gusting down the telephone as he disconnected and a sudden thought struck him that the man on the end of the phone could be Peter Starling. A long shot, and not for him to speculate, especially as Mr Starling had every right now to return to his home.

This was just the sort of thing best kept to himself thought the solicitor as he immediately telephoned his client to inform her that there was another party interested in a future lease on the bakery. The people there now with experience of the job of baking had tentatively taken it on for six months just to see if they could cope and make a go of it; it could be that they would relinquish the bakery after six months, so he would ensure his client had another prospect.

If he was the missing husband, well, sooner or later they would have to meet to sort out all the problems and then he was pretty sure he'd soon be put in the picture. They would need his services to straighten it all out. That was the fascination of this job, he had always found, and smiled with satisfaction.

"Mrs Starling? Would you be interested in meeting a Mr Green who is very keen to consult you on the possibility of the leasing out of the bakery, should it become vacant after the remaining few weeks?"

Chapter 42

A persistent Mr Green, aided by Mr Timothy, who was enticed by the thought of future business, convinced Sally that she should meet the man. She could then consider renewing the bakery lease in his favour. If the present incumbents wanted to move on after the initial six months, she might not find someone immediately to carry on, and she was happily surprised at the way the bank balance she had set up for Peter was mounting. The belt and braces principle might be a good one to employ.

Mr Timothy would not divulge to Mr Green Sally's whereabouts, but was quite willing to pass messages back and forth. Moreover, he was almost sure, from the tone of the conversations, that the anxious caller was Mrs Starling's missing husband. Whether Mr Starling knew he was no longer a wanted man, Mr Timothy had no way of knowing and, discretion his watchword, would not attempt to meddle just to satisfy his curiosity. He would surely find out in good time.

Mr Timothy relayed the message to Mr Green that Mrs Starling would be taking the bus to Colchester the following Saturday to shop and would be available to meet him in the café by the bus station at 11 a.m. Could he make this appointment? Peter, phoning in from the call box yet again, sighed with relief now he had made contact and resolved to cycle there rather than catch a bus himself. He did not want to risk being trapped in a bus seat with someone who recognised him. There were only one or two buses into town on a Saturday and most of the villagers who wanted to shop on their only free day would take one of those. He would have to set out at nine o'clock to be sure to keep the appointment.

Old Partridge had given Peter an old fashioned look as he spruced himself up and climbed into clean clothes. Beyond announcing to him that he owed him for a couple of pints, Partridge kept silent. It had started when he had collected a letter on Peter's behalf addressed to a Mr Green, c/o The Marlborough in the High Street from a bemused landlord. Seth Skinner had known old Partridge for years and simply handed over the expected letter, wondering what he was up to this time. Probably something to do with all the coming and going of the casual help he had down there by the river.

"I do hope this'll be the last of 'em, mate, whatever you're up to," said Seth, poking a finger at the letter. He wasn't too worried. He'd never heard a bad word about old Partridge for all his unconventional life.

Partridge reluctantly counted enough pennies into his hand to buy the landlord and himself a pint and winked as he raised his glass to him. "Something I owe," he said, remembering the day of the storm and Peter's part in rescuing the boats.

As soon as Partridge presented the letter to Peter, he had started to fidget. Partridge's long mouth stretched down. He knew the signs; the boy was poised for flight, he shouldn't wonder. He wouldn't break the habit of a lifetime by asking Peter where he was going. It was better he didn't know anything more than he needed about his casual help.

Peter was sitting quietly at the back of the café, sideways on to the entrance, when Sally walked in. She looked from side to side before gasping as she saw him slowly turn towards her. She was not the only one shocked as he beheld her very rounded figure. Quickly, before either of them could comment, Sally walked over and sat down heavily at the table. "You!" was all she could say.

There were many overtures Peter had considered to start an amicable (he hoped) conversation with Sally to find out what was happening, but the sight of her obvious fecundity, had him thrown into confusion. Slow to gather his wits, Sally was quicker with, "Some joke, you're pulling, to turn up here out of the blue after all this time!"

How could she think he'd planned such a frivolous thing? The consequences were catastrophic if he was caught. "A joke? You call this a joke? I risk my neck to find out if you're all right – and I can quite see you are – and you say it's a joke?"

Risk his neck? What was all that about? Sally gasped, "Peter...."

"So what game has my wife been playing now?" he asked, indicating the region of her stomach across the table.

Instantly stirred to retaliation, Sally rounded on him, "You forfeited any rights to call yourself my husband when you shot Jim – shooting him!" she repeated on an incredulous rising note.

"Keep your voice down – would you really want to turn me in?" Peter hissed.

And then she knew he was unaware of his luck, that Jim would not make charges against him. So this was why he'd been out of touch, no one knowing where he was. It had never occurred to her that word would not reach him. All this time, for four whole months, he had lived in fear of being arrested for wounding Jim... or even murder! But what was he saying now? "...Got what he wants, my wife ... child on the way..."

"Peter, Peter! No one's after you. No one wants you arrested." She was appalled that he had been unaware of this for so long.

He stopped in mid-sentence and leaned across the table, holding Sally with his eyes. "What – Why?" Then slowly he subsided into his seat again, head moving down and away, wary of a trick. Sally was so obviously lost to him now, he felt he no longer knew her, much less trusted her word.

"Jim was wounded in the shoulder," then seeing Peter slump back. "You thought you'd killed him?"

Just a feeble nod from Peter, then a groan, eyes closed.

"He was in hospital for almost two weeks," she

185

continued. "We didn't know where you'd gone. Where did you go?" She watched as Peter lifted a desultory hand and let it fall back on the table edge.

"Peter... he wouldn't press charges. Not in the circum –" Suddenly, she had lost her voice and leaned back in her chair, momentarily overcome by the enormity of it all. Peter running away and having to hide all this time, thinking he might be caught and hanged. She had been so worried, wondering where he was. She watched his face as he digested the news, feeling sorry about everything.

As he slowly considered the implications, the whole mess, his voice low and anguished, he asked, "How could you have done it, Sally? We had so much together."

Sally regarded him with pity and some remorse, but rallying, said crisply, "What's done is done, Peter. You know there's no going back. The money from the bakery; it's saved for you, in an account in your name..."

"I'll be back at the bakery you know," he interrupted.

"You can't..."

"Can't, Can't? Christ, it's my bloody bakery! Sorry it would inconvenience you to have me back living near you. You cleared off don't forget – and now look at you – wouldn't sleep with me, but you carry another man's child! Don't you tell me what I can't do!"

Sally looked round and was glad to see they were still alone in the café; the proprietor had stepped smartly into the back kitchen as soon as their voices were raised. He didn't want to be near any trouble.

"Still the volatile Peter – no wonder I'd had enough!" Then more gently, "Peter, it would help if we could talk calmly. You must see that this mess ought to be cleared up. Thank God you now know you're free to come and go, at least I could tell you that."

"Just because bloody old Macaulay's talked the police into dropping the charges, don't think I'm too grateful. It was you and that charming bastard you've taken up with who got me into trouble in the first place!" All the same, Peter's relief, his gradual unwinding and relaxing as he began to realise he was free again, was unmistakable.

"There's no point in our continuing this conversation – if you can call it that," said Sally sharply. "It seems you have contacted Mr Timothy, so we can negotiate through him," and softer, "What do you say, Peter?" Sally realised at last that she'd become immune to the acrimony with Peter and just wanted to get back home to the even tenor of life with Jim. "There will be more to discuss when you have thought longer about the future, now you know you're not a wanted man."

Sally rose slowly from the chair with her hands flat on the table, mauve mottled as they pressed down to support her growing weight. Peter looked across at them, to the hands of a stranger wearing a different ring from the one he had given her. He raised his eyes to the woman he had known and loved for so long, surprised that he didn't want to reach out to those hands, nor to keep her there any longer. Incredibly, this woman was still his wife, but how cold and distant she now was. The door of the café swished closed behind her and she was gone.

He sank back with his head in his hands and mulled over the shattering implications of this meeting. How everything had changed so quickly from this morning. Even if he had begun to feel free of the woman he now perceived Sally had become, it was still too soon for him to shake off the shackled feelings of a hunted man.

Chapter 43

Trixie was up early on this bright May morning. She began to laugh as she watched the good mother hen she'd kept from last year to go broody. The hen flapped and clucked with alarm as she forbade her nine goslings to paddle in that nasty cold water swilling about beneath the outside tap. Careful not to name her chickens – they didn't stay for long so she hated to get too fond of them – Trixie had nevertheless named Daisy, white with beautiful black feather markings round her throat. She had put ten fertile duck eggs under her when she would not move from the nest. Trixie determined not to do it again. The poor hen, much better at keeping an eye on the ducklings than any duck mother, was distraught at the antics of her hooligan brood. She'd never seen anything like it in her life! If they weren't sloshing about in puddles they were making muddy tracks across the just-ploughed field beside the smallholding. They ran about in the rain piping with delight, and wouldn't take a scrap of notice of her clucking. Trixie saw the poor Daisy reduced to skin and bone, while the ratio of ducklings was unlucky; six males to three females and one failed to hatch. She would have to swap a good few of the drakes when they had grown, probably for some more chickens, a much better bargain.

She turned to the lean-to by Tolly's converted shed and pulled him a good haynet. As she walked to Tolly's loose box a movement caught her eye. She was astonished to see Peter walking diffidently up the path. She stood with the hay bundle cradled in both arms and stared at him, not knowing how to react.

"Trixie..." he began.

"You've turned up like the proverbial bad penny after all

188

this time!" Trixie said hotly.

"I have wanted to call for a long time, just to thank you and ask your forgiveness, but I had to pluck up enough courage…"

"You hoodwinked me, and with such a straight face," she shot back.

"I'm sorry, I really am, as much for conning you as anything. Trixie, I was desperate and frightened. I didn't know what to do. It was never planned," he reddened and looked at his feet as he talked, like a small boy caught out.

"So, you've come back after all this time to apologise?" she asked, watching his face above the hay she still held. "You must know I had to hand in the shotgun. The police were here the day after, you know."

"I thought I might have killed old Macaulay, but I never meant to do such a thing. I thought I might have hanged!" He looked into her eyes with pleading. "I had to lie to you; and you wouldn't have wanted to know the truth!"

Tolly walked round his confined space, waiting for his hay.

"I understand now. Everyone knows what's been going on, of course, but I was very worried at the time where you'd gone, and my hand in it," Trixie recalled.

Tolly circled yet again while he waited for his hay, then poked his neat little grey muzzle up over the door and whickered. She didn't usually tease him in this way. Quickly, Trixie relinquished her tight hold on the netted hay and opened Tolly's door to tie it on the ring. This short interval gave her time to think about what Peter had said. Peter followed her and looked over the door. Tolly rolled his eyes back and got his nose in the hay. "About time too," said his expression. He stamped his foot in irritation. Men were always trouble, he found, though George was the one exception.

Trixie shrugged as she closed Tolly's half-door again. How could anyone know the true circumstances of anyone else's marriage? But she had seen the effect it had on Peter, driven to extremes by Sally's defection. She did not doubt for one moment his desperation at the time. Her sympathies lay with him.

"Well, if you've come to mend fences, there are plenty here to mend," she said half-jokingly.

"What did the police ask you?" he ventured as he followed her round while she fed and inspected the stock.

"They asked me where I'd dropped you off, they wanted your shotgun, and when the whole business came out, I realised by the Sergeant's manner that they were quite sure you'd shot him. I was appalled at my part in it. Where did you go?"

In the telling, they both gradually relaxed in each other's company. Trixie heated some soup and they ate together. Both were thankful for the fortunate outcome and that Peter would soon be able to take up where he left off at the bakery. Peter was momentarily silenced by the thought of returning to where he had worked for so long with Sally. It would be different, lonely, now he faced the thought.

"I'll get some help in again, start back into baking. It's the most useful job I can do, although I'm quite good at painting boats, too." He lifted a hand, rough now, with the wear of outdoor life. "My hands have never been the same since," he added, in the high tone of a fussy housewife. He folded his hand down as if for her inspection and rolled his eyes.

Such an unnatural action looked ludicrous in a man so big and obviously masculine, and she laughed across the small room at him.

"It's good to see you smile again, Trixie," he said, pleased.

"I see so few people day-to-day here where it's off the beaten track that, unless the animals have a barmy half-hour, I forget to laugh. I've got used to being rather insular and alone. I'll be a hermit if I don't watch out!" She spoke lightly but the thought did not please her.

"Would you let me make it up to you, my deception, I

mean? It will be a month or two before I can regain the bakery, but I'm staying at The Marlborough for now, kicking my heels until I can get started again. I'm getting bored, not used to lounging about. You could do with a hand on the digging," he said quickly as he saw her face cloud over.

Trixie, suddenly doubtful, said "You know tongues will wag if you're seen around here too often, don't you. I don't have to tell you that I already have a bit of a reputation for going my own way, wearing trousers and all. Dear me! But that would be as nothing as to what they'd say if you, not yet divorced, and me the older woman were seen too much together. Don't forget, it was me who helped you make your escape! Then, suddenly aggrieved again, "And in all innocence, too."

Peter was silent. He'd made a shaky truce today and now he must tactfully make himself scarce. As he left, he called back, "Think about it, Trixie. You can tell them you're hiring me to help if you like, though I won't take a penny. I have enough coming in from the lease on the bakery." And with that he was gone, leaving Trixie to make up her own mind.

Thereafter, at one end of the Settlement, Peter was seen to be employed by Trixie, going back and forth from The Marlborough to help her with the last spring planting and to catch up on some neglected maintenance on the smallholding.

Fortunately, the Wooden Fender lay along the road right at the other end of the village.

Chapter 44

The Coronation celebrations were early next month and most of the community were putting great effort into making the do up at the big hut a memorable one.

Since they had heard that the children would have to go to school that day and since the packing shed would be open too and most of the men working, it was decided to schedule the community celebrations for the following Saturday. The whole day could be taken up with events, and everyone could join in.

Bella was busy making a huge fruit cake from her Christmas recipe, because it was the likeliest to keep for the week or two. Unless the little shop could spare some room in its freezer, there wasn't a lot she and the other wives could do in advance to put a big tea party together for the younger children. Benny said he would mention it when he was calling next on the Browns, and he was sure they would help if they could. Benny was delighted to earn a smile from Bella for this suggestion. She was usually so distant with him.

She and Tom had a secret and she was telling no one, least of all that gossip Benny. Like a good few neighbours who had been dithering on the brink of getting a television, the thought of being able to see the Coronation as the day progressed, although they were miles away from the unique occasion, persuaded Bella and Tom. They had arranged for a television to be delivered in time for the Coronation. Once it was installed, they would invite anyone who wanted to squash into their living room to see it with them. She was more excited by this thought than anything else right now.

The men were getting organised on some fireworks for the Saturday evening, but if the children were to see them they'd have to let them off in the daylight she thought, or the little ones would be asleep before the late darkness of a long June day.

The packing shed was to be cleared, a huge task involving the removal of the noisy banks of rollers which usually carried along the produce to be graded by the women. Then the chip baskets were stacked at one end or under cover outside, and the forklift trucks took pallets and everything else too heavy for the men to lift on their own outside. The great empty shed looked the size of an aircraft hangar, dead and alien after the usual noise and bustle. Then rows of rough trestle tables were laid along the big shed's sides and wrapping paper utilised to cover them for the children's competitions. These were to be made small and simple in the hope that all the children would be encouraged to take part. This would make it easier for the judges to ensure each child received at least a Coronation mug and perhaps a five-shilling commemorative crown in its small plastic box.

Some of the women were stringing together bright triangular scraps of cloth to make bunting to drape above the shed entrance. Young and old on the Settlement seemed to be working on some project to make a memorable day for them all. All they needed now was some good weather, so they could have a tea party on the lawn in front of the packing shed instead of inside the hut where there would be a dance for the adults later in the evening after the fireworks.

A small army of wives had undertaken to polish the tired wooden floor of the hut which had suffered the scrapes of too many chair legs and boots. Each lady knelt line abreast at the furthest end from the door and began working down. Benny, having finished his postal deliveries, stuck his head round the door with the intention of practising on the piano before the big day. Fascinated, he beheld the tidal wave of ever advancing females, behinds swaying in rhythm as they worked. The sight had him dithering in confusion. He began backing quietly away. Wild horses couldn't get him up on the stage to play the piano in front of – or, in fact, behind – these

193

ladies today. They would tease him as mercilessly as they teased some of the packing shed foremen when they all got together. Just as he thought he'd got safely clear without detection, Jean arrived carrying a bucket of cleaning materials and he backed straight into her.

"Now what are you up to, my lad?" she asked, more joking than severe.

She always seemed to wrong-foot him, the woman he so admired. His face grew redder as he shyly considered an explanation, then simply gave up, tongue-tied, and fled.

Jean looked after him, perplexed, then chuckled as, with sudden insight, she thought it high time he met a good woman who could sort him out.

Chapter 45

As the day of the Coronation celebrations came closer, Peter watched the flurry around him while the preparations were made. He had finally become used to being a free man, coming and going, helping Trixie, who appreciated an extra pair of hands. He had the sympathy of many of his male acquaintances for meting out rough justice, as they saw it. Not many knew how they would have acted in Peter's place. Just as well Jim Macaulay didn't press charges, especially when that Sally was well on the way with carrying his child.

Trixie did her usual gallop about the smallholding, working well into the evenings of the long summer days when she could get ahead with maintenance, having Peter's sure help.

"Will you be going to the fête on Saturday?" asked Peter finally, having wondered for days if he would ever pluck up courage to ask her to go with him.

"Elsie has asked if I would go with her and her family. I was going to call in to them on the way," she replied, setting down tea and slices of apple cake for their elevenses.

"There's a dance in the evening." He picked up a spade and stared at it.

"Yes, I know," she said. "I don't know whether I still can dance. I haven't thought about such a thing for years!"

"Course you can. It's like riding a bike, you never forget. I'd like us to go together… please. I could be your escort. What do you say?" Having started and unwound his tongue at last, he could hardly stop. The tea was cooling, the cake sat untouched.

Needing time to get used to the question, she said diffidently, "I can't ride a bike." Then, "Do you know, I doubt I have a dress fit to wear. My only dress, that is." She was suddenly diverted by this admission. "I bet it's got the moth!" And, not stopping to give him an answer, she turned and sprinted into the house and upstairs. He was left shaking his head. Well, at least he'd got as far as asking her.

She returned more slowly, holding the green cotton dress with its wide, white collar doubtfully up to her front, muddy boots and trouser bottoms sticking out below, her small, sun-touched face framed by dark tangles, hay flecks crowning the whole effect. "Cinderella could never go to the ball in this little rig-out. Heaven knows, I've never needed any clothing coupons to go towards new dresses these last few years," she added ruefully.

She had, in fact, bolted off to give herself time to reflect on his offer to take her to the dance. Lately, she had realised more and more that she had cut herself off from much of the social life of the Settlement. The Coronation fête would be a good launch to get her back into the swim of things, and she would really enjoy kicking up her heels at a dance for a change. It was about time she took herself in hand and had a long overdue evening out with friends; it would be something to look forward to. But… "Will you give me a day or two to think about it, Peter? Are you sure you want to spend the evening with this old lady – and what about the gossip?"

He was amazed that it had got so complicated. "Wear that dress, it's OK. What's wrong with it? Look, I'm just asking you if we should go to the dance together, that's all."

"Oh, I know what you're asking," she said quietly looking up at him. "I just don't think you do." He looked bewildered.

Next day, Trixie took herself off to see Elsie at about 10.30am when she'd finished her morning jobs. Elsie fished out a bottle of coffee and poured a teaspoonful in each of two cups.

"This is an honour, Mrs Langham," said Elsie happily, as they sat each side of the scrubbed white kitchen table.

"There's a catch," Trixie replied jokingly. Then, "Elsie,

Peter has asked me to go to the dance with him on Saturday. What do you think about it? Should I go?"

"It's high time you got out a bit, girl," replied Elsie stoutly, but she knew why Trixie hesitated. "When did you worry about gossip?" she added perceptively, then, "Why don't you both call in to us and we'll all four go together? Flo says she'll sit in with the children." Flo was Alan's elderly mother.

Trixie could have hugged her, but shyly muttered "Thank you, Elsie," and took another sip of coffee to hide her face for a moment. "I'll just have to get a new dress. My old green one has seen better days – and I don't want to look like mutton... you know!"

Elsie laughed. "Don't worry about being seen out with Peter, Trixie, no one will recognise you anyway by the sound of it, you in a dress for a change!"

"I'll have to go to Manningtree and while I'm there, I must get this hair cut; I'll never get my hands looking respectable in time!" Trixie whirled as she rose to her feet and, thanking her friend once again, made for the door.

Elsie hadn't seen Trixie so bubbling for a long while, and she smiled as she watched her stepping lightly down the wide path. Walter would have been proud of her, the way she'd got to grips with their smallholding these past four years. It was a tonic to see Trixie coming out of hiding again. What if something more permanent came of it? It was true there was all of five years difference in age between Trixie and Peter – and the wrong way round as far as some would have it, though hardly as far as cradle–snatching.

In this close community it was all very well saying gossip didn't matter, but it was a lonely life if neighbours didn't get on. Annie Morgan would be in her element if she saw Trixie and Peter dance a step together and Peter not yet divorced, though Elsie knew Mr Timothy had it in hand. Every community had an Annie and everyone knew who their Annie was. Elsie laughed and crossed her fingers, hoping it would all come right. From what she'd seen on the few occasions she had called on Trixie, Peter seemed to have taken well to the outdoor life and Trixie looked happy in his company. She ran ahead in her mind: could the time come when Peter decided he did not want to work again at the bakery? Now that would be a turn about... Elsie smiled at the thought.

Chapter 46

The day of the Coronation dawned disappointingly wet. Not even enough blue for a baby's bib, thought Bella, never mind a pair of sailor's trousers! Although Bella was out of bed at 6.30 a.m., Tom had risen even earlier to get started on his morning's work. As he'd got older, he'd found the midday heat of some sunny June days while he was bouncing about on the hard iron seat of the Ferguson was beginning to tell. Although he always wore his cap, the open cab left him exposed to all weathers. The seasons shaped their days, but the weather always dictated how the job was done. Today he'd had to find his old fawn raincoat. Why did it always seem to rain in the first week of June when hay making was about to start?

Tom and Bella's bedroom was large, stretching from the front of the semi-detached house to the back with windows either side. Bella stepped onto the blue rag rug beside the bed and walked to the front window to look out across the field. She saw the train smoke white and billowing in the pale early light cutting across the width of the window. The energetic puffing and chugging of the unseen engine made a short, hollow echo as it went under the small red bridge. She had always been lulled by this sound, distant and infrequent enough to be pleasing. It was one of the comforting sounds of home.

She leaned her elbows on the windowsill in a rare moment of reflection. Life was so much easier for them all in the summer months, an unconscious slowing down; a blessed contrast with the hurried winter bustle to get through the chores in daylight while trying to keep warm.

Since she'd had an immersion heater in the kitchen along

with her modern little grey Jackson cooker, there was no need for sweltering summer fires in the range. The other big summer blessing was that the washing dried without the need to drape it wetly over every available space indoors, the most miserable discomfort on a cold, rainy day. No one looked forward to summer more than she did, even if today of all days looked as if it was going to be wet without relief.

She hugged this small quiet time to herself before her feet, cool on the lino a moment ago, began to feel chilly. She turned to the huge pine chest of drawers (so big that when they moved in it had to be carted upstairs in two cut halves) and took off her hairnet to place in the little dish she kept there with her hairpins. She had once kept water overnight in the large jug here for an early morning cold splash, just as her Spartan mother had. Now there was just she and Tom at home she had time and space to use the kitchen sink and have the luxury of a warm kettle-full of water.

Still standing by the window, she continued to mull over the possibilities of the day just started. Then, with a small, girlish squeal, she remembered the hat, and ran to her wardrobe where it had been sitting on top like a forgotten dream. Slowly, she unwrapped it from paper crisp and flaking with age, and lifted out the still-pristine hat which had nestled there since VE Day. It had been proudly worn, but since then there had been no occasion to wear such a frivolous creation. Her life was just not geared to dressing up. She smiled as she knelt on the floor holding the brim. What if she had worn it to visit the shop on her bicycle, or even into town? The neighbours would have thought she'd gone mad. Or had a fancy man! If she carefully cut off the veil with its little black v's, she would update it enough to wear on Saturday to the celebrations.

Carefully, she placed the hat on the bed and turning, the swept fireplace caught her eye. She tutted at the sight of some fawn-coloured billywitches lying dustily dead in the hearth. Every June, dozens of these heavy bugs droned down the chimney and were too stupid to find their way out of an open window. They would have to stay there for now. There was so much to get ready this morning.

The opaque grey eye of a television receiver stared at her when she opened the stair door into the living room. She wondered if she would ever get used to it sitting there, intrusively, in her home. It simply didn't look as if it belonged, perched like that on the sideboard.

The grandchildren had already seen some programmes and thought it a huge treat. Barry had been utterly enthralled watching a programme on Africa. It was the size of the animals shown on a safari that had amazed him, the unexpected, unimagined power of them. Simply being told how big a wild animal was could not be the same. Books were not enough. She was a little more comfortable with the cold-eyed monster she had in her living room if it brought a wider knowledge of the world to them. It was frightening how the time went by while they had the thing switched on, but then it was very new. She had thought at first it would be just like the wireless when the novelty had worn off, but now had begun to think differently.

Chapter 47

It was a toss-up whether to leave a standing space as people came and went or to allow more chairs for comfort. Bella deliberated as she gathered all the chairs she could to line up in her small living room. She put round plenty of dishes to do duty for ashtrays. Once, when the chimney caught fire, she'd had firemen round and was loath to repeat the experience.

It was still a working day for most and Tom was at one of the hay barns using the tractor to move last year's bales to one side to allow room for the new cut hay. She hoped he'd not be too long as he'd be sure to be hot and dusty and want a good wash-down at the sink. From the airing cupboard, she took a block of green soap and a new round tin of toothpaste. There were some clean clothes for him on one of the kitchen chairs. He'd be a bit put out if he had to negotiate his own living room full of visitors with hardly a stitch on, to get to the stairs and the haven of their bedroom. Tom always appreciated such attention and it would put him in the right frame of mind to play host, something she could not remember their ever doing on such a scale, in all the years they'd live there. Friends calling always made her wonder if they'd ever have a bathroom and inside flush lavatory like the Joneses and Jean and Bob. It had to happen one day, before she reached her 60s, she hoped.

What would it be like with a Queen on the throne instead of a King? She couldn't see that it would make much difference to them, but from photographs she had seen of Princess Elizabeth when she was smiling, she thought her face looked warm and friendly and fancied that she might herald a happy new era for Britain. There was the hope that everyone might finally be leaving the aftermath of the war years, as well as rationing, firmly in the past. Most people she knew had felt very sorry for the King, struggling to do well the job thrust upon him, and having to make speeches, with such difficulty, into the bargain.

Bella switched on the television to warm up and dusted the magnifying glass across the small screen just as Tom came through the five-bar gate on the Ferguson. The screen buzzed angrily and a storm of snow-white static zipped across it in bands until Tom switched off the tractor motor. It was only occasionally that cars went along the Harwich Road and started off these blizzards but Bella thought it always seemed to be at the most interesting part of a programme and she couldn't hear a word until it cleared.

Jean and Bob were getting ready to slip across the road to see the television with Bella and Tom when a distraught Jim Macaulay banged on their door. Agitatedly, he told them that Sally had gone into labour and while the district nurse was with her he had come to see if they would go back with him in the van.

"But, but it's ages yet," Jean said, slow and puzzled. Then she gathered herself and started what Bob referred to as a 'spin' as she looked round to see what she might need to take.

"Just leave everything and come," urged Bob and shepherded her past the two Labradors who had woken from deep snoring in their beds and lumbered to their feet to stand blocking the door waiting for it to open. "No such luck, you two," said Bob as he pushed them out of the way and guided Jean in front of him out to the van.

Tom drew the curtains in the kitchen to strip off his shirt for a wash. Just as he was emerging from over the bowl of hot

203

water, Bob rapped hard on the back door and Tom heard him explaining to Bella about the baby. He looked up with a soapy face, water streaming from his elbows, to call out, "Good luck, Bob, we'll wet the baby's head later," through the closed kitchen door.

Tom slipped upstairs to change into his smartest clothes and Bella left the back door open. George's wife, Violet stepped hesitantly across the doorway. "Oh, Vi, I'm glad you're here first, it gives me a chance to ask how George is doing with the horses. Here have a cup of tea before the pot needs filling again. Tom hasn't long been in."

Violet found a chair by the window and said, "George reckons it works a treat this time of year with all the grass about and the two of them living out, so long as he watches the pasture. They don't need too much good grass, not working like."

Annie came in next, followed by Fred, whose straight grey hair was streaked back hard either side of his ears and plastered down with water. His cap, which he never left home without, was held before him in both hands like a supplication for peace, as he followed in her wake. He looked as if he'd got his orders this morning, thought Tom, somewhat spruce himself, what with all the company today. He passed Fred a glass of beer from a few he'd put by in the kitchen. Fred looked a great deal happier as he grinned his thanks at Tom and went to sit by Annie.

Bella greeted Gwen at the door, who'd left Toby looking after Gwyneth, and settled her by Violet with tea and a piece of chocolate cake. "Toby says he'll slip down for a spell when I get back later," said Gwen on a happy sigh. Just getting out of the house was, for her, a rare event, and then there was the company, and the Coronation to see on television. Bella, who had been wondering how the day would go and if they had enough room and could cope, forgot her slight nervousness and began to enjoy it with the rest of them. The scent of sweetpeas drifted from the bunch she'd picked from her garden that morning, as the women fell to discussing the fashions and the guests waiting for the coach carrying the future Queen to arrive at Westminster Abbey. The newspaper, already crinkled, was passed from hand to hand as each guest was identified, and the ladies exclaimed in frustration at the black and white pictures, longing to see the colour of it all.

George, who came in later, took a keen interest in the horses on the screen. He'd never seen so many in one place before. His beer stood untouched and his pipe sat idle in the middle of being filled while he took in the sight of the fine horses and carriages, a world away from his Hector and Fancy. And all that polished harness. He was mesmerised by the sight of the Queen of Tonga, smiling from her open top carriage in the downpour while a smart little man in uniform sat stoically by her side. The horses pulling their carriage looked well up to the weight and the uneven load. He'd never seen anything like it.

In between passing cups of tea and plates of sandwiches back and forth, Bella had time to wonder how Sally was faring. She missed Jean's company today, but was thrilled that Jean would at last have a grandchild. She knew how much it would mean to her and Bob and she would feel much freer to talk to Jean about her own grandchildren. They would have even more in common to talk about when they next met. She heard Gwen saying to Annie that they would try to buy a television for Gwyneth. Now that was a good idea.

As everyone was about to leave in mid-afternoon, Jean came rushing over. "Oh, I'm so glad I caught you all. It's a girl! Guess what, she's called Elizabeth!" Bella forgot herself so far as to give Jean a huge hug. Dodging around everyone now standing, talking animatedly, to find some sherry in the bottom of the sideboard, she caught sight of Annie's face, lips pressed straight. Now wasn't the time for Annie to give expression to her thoughts on an illegitimate baby. Bella caught her eye with a warning look and was grateful to see her look down and away. She poured the first sherry and passed the glass to Annie, who gave her a small smile as if to acknowledge that nothing should be allowed to spoil this neighbourly day. She continued to pour a sherry for each of the ladies and called across the room to Tom, "Tom, will you pour the men a drink and we can have at toast?" He signalled he'd heard and poured each man a glass of beer. This would set the seal on a very happy day for them all.

"Raise your glasses to toast the future!" Tom exclaimed.

"And another to little Elizabeth!" returned Bella and the ladies.

Chapter 48

At the Wooden Fender, Nurse Crombie's presence filled the little bedroom with brittle purpose, intolerant of anything and anyone who might distract her from 'mother', as she quaintly addressed Sally. Her attitude demanded that prospective grandparents, but particularly fathers, would be most useful downstairs out of the way. The doctor had been informed that Sally was in labour and had laconically replied that he would be along soon enough. After all, Nurse Crombie was in charge, as efficient a midwife as he'd ever met.

Jim cast a worried glance over his shoulder as he was ushered out behind Jean and Bob. Sally looked so small and lost in the pillows of their bed.

Downstairs, Jean had time to reflect as she cast a guarded look at Jim across the room. She could not overcome her reserve, although she could see how happy her daughter was with him, and he with her. She did not approve in the slightest Sally leaving her husband, much less setting up at the pub with Jim. Try as she might, Jean could not hide her disappointment. There was a coolness between mother and daughter that had never been there before. She had got on very well with Peter; saw him as a caring, faithful, hard-working man – a good enough husband for any woman – and couldn't understand why Sally went astray. She was, however, much more tolerant of Jim when she had heard about the shooting and that Jim would not pursue the matter with Peter. How could Peter have been so stupid and where was he now? Working (they said) for that Trixie and her menagerie, that's where! Didn't Sally care? It had been a confusing, worrying time, and now this. She prayed silently that it would soon be over and that Sally and the baby would be all right.

She shot a glance at Bob, sitting so affably across from Jim who was fidgeting and cocking his head at the ceiling. Did men accept these things more readily than women? Through it all, he had been far less critical than she and today he sat there stoically waiting for their first grandchild to arrive.

Restlessly, she got up and went into the kitchen. Seeing that it would benefit from a good clear-up and tidy (she knew where she was with that) she found Sally's pinafore and set to using up her nervous energy taking it out on the room. She'd make them all a cup of tea when she'd given the cups one of her wash-ups. Really, the whole place could do with a spring-clean. What was the matter with young girls these days?

Young Elizabeth Macaulay did not keep them waiting long. She arrived small and svelt as a little seal. Jim leaped upstairs when he heard the baby's cry. Wordlessly, he knelt and put his head on the pillow beside Sally and simply gazed at her, his worried expression changing to a tender smile. He thought she would look wan and tired but she seemed buoyed up with excitement and happiness. Her exuberance was momentarily stilled as she reached across the small space between them to touch his face, now rough with a new day's beard.

"Fancy our baby being born today. Coronation Day, Jim. The Queen cannot be happier than I am right now!"

Jim found his voice at last, "Clever as well as beautiful," he said simply and sincerely. A snuffle came from the wooden cot set on rockers. Smiling, Jim rose and crossed the room. He stood, just looking down at the small, red-faced baby lying with eyes closed, mouth animated and questing, while his world slowed enough for him to take in the fact that here was his daughter. Their daughter! Gently, he scooped her up, his long hands holding her closely wrapped in the soft, white cover. "Little love," he whispered, and kissed her. Finally, with a big, thankful sigh, he carried her to Sally's open arms, then walked steadily downstairs to call Jean and Bob to come and see their first grandchild.

Chapter 49

The great day of the Fête, planned for and eagerly awaited, dawned dry and fair, much to the relief of all. The outdoor events could take place outdoors; they would not be curtailed or squashed in between the stalls in the big packing shed. Notwithstanding that today was a special national holiday, there would be a jumble sale. It would always be included whatever event the Settlement held. All was set for a once-in-a-lifetime occasion in the memory of most in the community.

The children's efforts, from paintings to strange animals assembled from awkward-looking vegetables to miniature flower arrangements in egg cups, were duly admired. Prizes of Coronation mugs and coins were awarded to include all the children in one way or another. Families wandered from stall to stall, the men bowling for one of the half-grown piglets, pounced on that morning and polished up for the occasion. This would be a worthwhile prize to add to those pigs already coming along in sties at home.

George drew up in the huge blue-painted hay wagon to give the youngsters and the not so young, rides round the grounds. Hector and Fancy stood tall and proud in spanking clean tack, well aware of the admiration coming their way. George watched, amused, as one or two of the children shyly advanced with odd pieces of food to offer the horses. Great long heads reached gently down to mumble crusts from tiny, outstretched hands, and the horses didn't move when tit bits fell to the floor and were offered again.

There were many tight-lipped ladies in close discussion after the judging of the home-made cakes and jams. These goodies would be donated to the tea later in the day. One or two had eyes in the direction of Annie's strawberry jam, this time sitting innocently at the end of a table.

The children's races in the afternoon were hugely popular – the sack race, the three-legged, the egg and spoon. All the age groups seemed to be revelling in their events. The announcement that the fathers should run a race came as no great surprise and they groaned good-naturedly as the course was swiftly extended to the furthest length. The ladies watched and cheered gleefully, animated, with their worries left at home. Hats, wildly bobbing up and down, were removed. Hair fell free from pins and tumbled unheeded. When the ladies' race followed, the men gallantly conceded that the course should be shorter. The ladies, their colour high, kicked off their shoes, disregarding precious nylons for once. Girlish giggles and nervous glances ensued until the 'go' sounded when, a latent spirit of competition suddenly awakened in them, skirts were picked up as the score or so of women in their prettiest dresses raced erratically to the finishing line. It was the men's turn to watch their ladies drifting down the field in the colours of butterflies, knees and petticoats, charmingly immodest, displayed as they advanced. Spurred on by this stirring sight, the men arrived first at the finishing tape. They claimed their ladies who, disarmed and breathless, fell against them and were steered smartly off to revive in the tea tent.

Soon, the young children sat together all round a long table set outside for tea, while the food kept coming: so much food. There were unlimited cakes and jellies after the obligatory sandwiches to start, and then full little tummies rested while the fireworks were set up. It was a day meant for the children to remember for many years afterwards, a day given to them out of ordinary life.

Chapter 50

Then there was the Dance in the evening. Trixie had raced round the whole smallholding settling all the stock down an hour earlier than usual. It had been as long ago as when Walter was alive that she'd been out to any kind of entertainment in the evening. That was when Walter would do his gallant best to whirl them round a dance floor, but his knee injury would curtail his efforts. Then they would sit on chairs and watch from the sidelines. But she had so loved to dance.

Sure as she was when dealing with the animals, she was all shaky and uncertain when it was time to get ready before Peter called. They were to walk to Elsie and Alan's and go on with them from there, but she was quite sure she would never get herself together in time.

If the boiler didn't buck up a bit and heat the water more quickly, she'd be caught in the kitchen still in the bath. She nervously closed the curtains on the bright evening just in case. She'd already washed her hair and rinsed it in warmed rainwater until it was soft and shining – not a hayseed to be seen. She'd soaked her hands in lemon juice to try to get rid of vegetable stains that, up to now, hadn't bothered her in the slightest. Her nails would never be anything but short and uneven; she'd just have to do her best with them. Looking as smart as she could would give her confidence, for she was feeling shy of suddenly finding herself in crowded company, having been on the edge of things for so long.

Finally, drying herself after her tepid bath, she ran her eyes round her little kitchen. This was a different world entirely from her young days in London, when dressing up to go out was such an everyday event. She suddenly stood quite still to reflect that never in a hundred years would she have guessed then that she would one day be living here on her small farm and getting ready to go out to spend the evening with a man other than Walter. Unconsciously, she rubbed one hand across her opposite forearm as if she'd felt a sudden chill, or the ache of a tender scar. "Walter," she whispered, "I'm going to a dance. With another man." How strange... she could not guess whether or not he would approve. The love was still there, easily recognised. She knew it always would be. His photograph was there on the windowsill, his face in black and white, untouchable under glass. Like her marriage, intangible, and complete.

Shaking herself, she hurried to put on her new outfit, a floral cotton dress with the new fuller skirt, practical sandals (for the walk and as well as dancing) over nylons eased on with trepidation. They were her only pair. It would have been an embarrassment if they'd laddered, she could not have gone bare-legged. The unfamiliar feel of the stockings and of her new dress, together with the intentness of her evening preparations, made her suddenly very aware of her femininity and that she felt good in her new clothes.

Just as she was working up to another bout of nervousness, Peter knocked on the door and she leapt to open it. He was thoroughly unprepared for his own reaction at the sight of Trixie dressed up ready for the dance. The last time he'd seen her, she was nearly knee-deep in stable manure, shovelling vigorously.

Day after day, they had mainly worked in their own patches, meeting for elevenses or for a quick discussion, Trixie pushing tangled hair from her hot face to solemnly discuss the way they might tackle the next task. From their wary distances, shy in new circumstances, they slowly got used to working together. Gradually, they had become good friends. Nothing, though, had prepared him for the impact she now made.

Recovering quickly, he said, "You'll be the belle of the ball!" and extended his crook of his arm for her to take.

212

Benny the Postman of many parts, was calling all assembled into the Paul Jones when Trixie, Peter, Elsie and Alan arrived. The general shuffle as people took to the floor, ready to exchange partners during this dance all round the room, eased the way for Trixie and Peter to enter into the proceedings. Trixie remembered the steps as if she had been dancing all her life. Peter watched her give him a small wave as they danced from one partner to another. He resolved never to let her immerse herself in day-to-day farming again with no time to have fun, if he could help it. But, of course, Trixie, for so long having her own independence, would never tamely follow anyone's suggestions.

Alan claimed Trixie for the next dance, the gentleman's choice. Elsie greeted Bella, and left Peter sitting happily with his first pint of the evening. He thoughtfully watched the dancers, and Trixie in particular. Here was this live wire of a woman, looking younger than her years and as happy in his company, now, as he was in hers. And something more; watching her from day to day dauntlessly coping with awkward tasks, had made him feel respect as well as admiration. He enjoyed lifting some of the physical burdens from her, helping her about the farm and knowing how much he was appreciated in turn. That was it; at last he felt appreciated.

Slow down. He took a sip of beer. Why had Sally's image now drifted into his mind? He reminded himself that they had gone their separate ways. That had been made crystal clear at their last meeting. There was no going back.

The music ended. He saw Trixie's carefree smile at Alan and suddenly strode across the room to claim her, walk her protectively to a chair and then fetch her a drink from the bar.

Seated and looking about her shyly, Trixie saw them all assembled, from tall, thin Annie, dressed from head to ankle in pale blue, ('like a yard of pumpwater', her mother would have said) to, lo and behold, Grannie Cafferty!

Fully intending to get her and her legs to the do somehow, Grannie had nevertheless given Grandson Joe the usual run-around. When he suggested that the only way she could get to the hut would be if he took her on the back of his BSA motorbike, she was in her element. The fact that the motorbike was a fairly tame one, was of no consequence to Grannie, who was gleefully looking at the matter from all angles. "What if the weather swings round again, comes over doubtful and lands right on top of us?"

Joe struggled out of Grannie's fireside chair, where the worn seat she would not replace had sunk so far that the stuffing was nearly touching the floor, and strolled to the window. "Doesn't look like rain, Gran," he said.

"No, it might not now, but it may later. We could get drownded on the way home and I'll hold you responsible. Fancy taking me off on a motorbike at my age," Grannie said sternly, while enjoying the thought.

"You don't have to come, Gran, though you could borrow my mac. And," (biggest sacrifice) "my helmet," said Joe, trying not to sound weary.

"I didn't say I didn't want to come. Did I say that?" asked Grannie defensively.

"Well, then," said Joe with finality.

Grannie Cafferty was content. She had been sufficiently coaxed to don the tight leather motorcycle helmet before perching gamely on the back of her Grandson's new BSA Bantam with the promise of a Guinness or two at the end of it. Now her seldom-combed bundle of hair was sticking out behind her, (it would perfectly describe a 'shock of hair') after the short, giddy, ride to the village hut. Grannie, not caring a hoot for dishevelment during her first pillion ride on a motorcycle, sat down happily with her promised Guinness and took a triumphant sip. She looked about her as she set the glass down with a "Well, I never..." as she spied Trixie with Peter.

Peter's attention to Trixie was not lost on many there, and there were many thoughtful looks, some amused and some questioning. It was certainly not lost on Annie, especially the way he looked at Trixie. 'Infatuated', she'd call it. Annie was still wearing the new hat she'd bought in honour of the fête, leaving the faithful, long-serving black hat at home for the first holiday of its life from a do at the hut. It had been deserted for a red tam-o'-shanter, clinging on with pins to her uncertain hairstyle, but Annie felt neat and controlled, and in tune with the older, more staid ladies present, also hatted.

She felt very patriotic in her blue dress and red hat and wished she could produce her white hanky to set off the whole effect but it had to be tucked into her knickers. The blue dress, locked in the utility era, had no pockets. She'd visit the ladies and fish it out if she needed a good blow.

Turning to the woman sitting next to her at the edge of the dance floor she whispered, but loudly, "It's a disgrace, him not divorced and her older by a mile. What do they think they're playing at?" Jane Saunders compressed her lips but kept silent. She had enough skeletons rattling too loudly in her own cupboard to hear anyone else's.

George glanced up at the remark. He had a soft spot for Trixie and admired her determination to work on at the smallholding. What was it to Annie or anyone if these two could start afresh and make each other happy? Someone had to get Annie out of her stays before trouble began! It wouldn't be Fred. He stood to lose too much. As it was, he was wandering around bereft of his cap, didn't know what to do with his hands unless he had them round a pint of beer.

George sighed in his corner and shuffled in his shoes, newly soled for the occasion. He reckoned he'd got the leather a little too narrow on the hob-iron for comfort. They'd have to be broken in – they did slip about on this floor. If he wasn't the oldest inhabitant, he felt it. All day he'd been helping families into, and out of, the wagon. He'd taken Hector and Fancy home, dragged off the heavy harness and brushed, fed and watered them. Only a lifetime of hard physical work had befitted him to keep going. Then, he didn't know whether some of them were more shocked by Peter turning up with Trixie or Annie going in for a new hat. He stirred and put down his half-finished pint. Leading the dance in a sprightly step wasn't his choice, but needs must when the devil, in the shape of Annie, was driving.

With a wink to Violet, sitting with Bella, her dear round face framed with silver hair, nodding back, he strode over to Annie and invited her to step with him in an easy waltz, just about to begin.

Together, faces straight, they shuffled in diffident steps once round the hall, unfamiliar at dancing with each other until George opened with, "Funny how things work out, Annie. Those two over there," he indicated with his head as he spoke, "have had lots against them. It might be a godsend now if they can take what life has given them and turn it to good for them both."

Annie suddenly pulled to a stop, a foot inadvertently planted on one of George's. "I know what you're up to, George Springett!" she hissed. "Don't you come holier than thou with me. Don't forget I help with the little ones in Sunday School. Fat lot of good it does to teach them what I know of right from wrong. Then we hold socials where a married man (who could easily have been a jailbird) turns up with an older widow, who never knew how to toe the line, always tearing about less than respectable!"

Once more grasping the long blue dress at approximately Annie's waist, George moved her off again as he tried a new tack. "I was going to ask you, when I saw you next, if you'll be wanting more of them there strawberries this year, Annie? They're coming along nicely and I know you made some good jam with them last year. I saw it in the autumn show. They make a good colour jam, girl, don't they?"

As he spoke, the change in Annie's face reminded him of a vixen he'd once seen caught in a snare. The small, sharp nose pointed straight at him, eyes watchful and defensive. Annie would rather have been caught robbing a bank than in this shameful little act. As the implication dawned and the colour began to rise from her thin neck, George felt contrite. Pleasure at his success in getting the words out without

216

bungling it, became tempered with compassion for her.

Then, wary of her sharp tongue, he swung Annie round before she could get a word in. But the day had taken its toll and his newly soled shoes went from under him. He crashed to the ground pulling Annie with him. Annie's red beret parted from her invisible hair net and pins scattered around as her hair came free. Her blue skirt belled round her thin, lisle-stockinged legs and her modesty was saved only by her long-legged, flesh-coloured knickers, white hanky waving out of the top like a flag of truce.

George yelped with a pain in one leg and then, tried to regain his feet and, weakly laughing, gave up the unequal struggle for the time being. Fred ambled over while the two still lay on the floor and put out a hand to help Annie up. "Well, you've let your hair down at last, Annie gal," he observed benignly and languid with beer, he put a comforting arm about her and led her to a seat at the edge of the floor to recover.

Benny called the next dance, a lively number to help speed the proceedings away from disaster, and most joined in. Violet went quietly over to join George now seated at the other side of the room, and Jack appeared to offer them a lift home.

It had been a grand day, thought Bella, just the way the whole Settlement could make it happen when they pulled together, and she was grateful that nothing had been allowed to spoil the occasion. It was fortunate that Sally was still lying in with little Elizabeth. She'd not be up and about for a few more days yet. It kept her and Jim occupied and safely away from possible trouble with Trixie and Peter. It seemed the situation there might well resolve itself in time. Sally and Jim could marry. She hoped so, for Jean and Bob's sake as well.

And what about the other two? Would something come of what she could now see was quite a friendship? She chuckled as she visualised the sparks which would undoubtedly fly if Peter tried to coerce Trixie to go his way, as she suspected he had with Sally. He'd be coping with some lively opposition there. There'd be more challenge than autocracy for Peter. That Trixie could hold her own with anyone.

Content with her day, she went to rummage for her coat hanging in the little room leading from the dance floor, then to prize Tom away from where he sat with Fred and Philbert Wright by the bar. Linking her arm through Tom's, she smiled up at him as they left. They did not need to use a torch. There was starlight enough to show them the way home.

Chapter 51

Sally slid seamlessly into motherhood as if it was what she had been waiting for all her life and old Jim Macaulay watching her as she cared for the baby, knew such joy that he felt he could shout to the world. With a new sense of purpose, he employed a school leaver to train as help in the bar, to allow Sally some leeway in her new role. There must have been a number of 'Elizabeths' born on Coronation Day, but none as beautiful as their daughter, and he would work to ensure that their Elizabeth had all they could provide. Jim Macaulay was a content and happy man.

A few weeks later, it was an unusually silent Sally who sat opposite Jim at breakfast. They had got to bed later than usual the night before after clearing up some of the debris of the evening session. Elizabeth had woken up more than once in the night and Sally had got up to feed and settle her again. Jim had offered to get started in the morning while she had a lie-in, but she felt too agitated to stay in bed and followed quietly on his heels into the kitchen.

Jim could see that Sally's edginess was more than just the result of her disturbed night. It was a long time since he'd seen her picking at the sleeve of her dressing gown. He watched her as he made some tea and set the toaster going, then pulled up a chair for her to sit, giving her shoulders an affectionate squeeze as she automatically sat down.

"This OK for you?" As he asked he passed her a jar of marmalade with a piece of toast.

"Mm – thanks." She distractedly pulled the plate towards her.

Jim waited, and picked up the daily paper with an air of unconcern.

"Jim- " breathlessly she paused. "Jim – little Elizabeth is such a good baby, isn't she." It was said as a statement.

What was coming? Thought Jim, trying to keep the paper still in his hands. He looked unconcerned as he replied "I think she is -"

"And you love her, don't you." Jim looked up from his paper astonished. Had he been giving young Elizabeth enough attention lately?

"Sally, did you want me to get up to her last night? I did offer – you only have to say. We can use a bottle or something, you know."

"No, it's not that love. It's just that, we've become very close; we live together, work together, tell each other everything." Sally was becoming even more agitated. "We do, don't we?"

Jim was getting worried now. The gods never seemed to let anything go right for very long without interference, he thought.

"Sally, tell me. Is Elizabeth all right?" He was halfway out of his chair, the paper falling on the floor.

Sally raised her palm to ease him back down into his chair again. "She's fine. All right. Jim, last night, when I got up to her, I put her back into her cot – she has a double-crown – her hair. The back of her head has a double crown just like Peter's!" She faced him, her last words rising in anguish. It was said and couldn't be unsaid.

Jim looked back at her quietly and directly, nothing in his expression giving away his thoughts. Thoughts that had drifted so smoothly into the knowledge that Elizabeth had not been his, but now she was. Like her mother; she had not been his but was now. He was not surprised at his ready acceptance. It was so simple. He loved them both.

"I have been worrying and wondering off and on," she continued looking down at her hands linked in front of her, "but now I'm sure, though it's so hard to believe; an eleventh hour baby, after all the years! And I had so wanted a child, for ages."

220

Suddenly, she rose to her feet. She could bear his silence no longer. "How can you sit there like that and say nothing!" she exploded. "If you want us to leave, say so and we'll go."

With outward calm, Jim sat back in his chair and picked up his paper again, holding the paper so steadily it didn't even rustle, and give away his fast heartbeat. "I always knew young Elizabeth Macaulay was Peter's," he said. "Right from the day she was born." (Well, not quite, but absolutely nothing was going to shake him from showing her his quiet acceptance.) "Was it wishful thinking that you couldn't see it, my darling?"

It was Sally's turn to look at Jim in astonishment. She took her cue from him and subsided while she said, "The changes that were going on during those dreadful weeks, when I wanted you so and couldn't see a way of telling Peter; I put them down to worry. The last thing I thought of in that little bedroom was that I could possibly be pregnant. It's just as she's grown, just fleeting moments, I've wondered – now I'm sure."

"I really didn't know whether you knew or not, Sally and frankly I don't care. I've been married before too, you know, and could well have had a ready family for you to look after. As it is, I've got a perfect little daughter whose mother, I hope, loves me as well as she does her, and I think she ought to go and pick her up in case she cries from neglect, and give us both a cuddle!" and he went back, with outward calm, to finish his toast, his head bent over the newspaper.

Sally sat stunned, taking this in. After all the wondering and worrying she'd been doing lately! How would he take the truth? Should she tell him – of course she must, such secrets had a way of surfacing. Tell him while she felt strong and with some control, instead of it springing at them later. Surely she would have to leave with little Elizabeth and start another new life. How many men would accept such bitter disappointment? Another man's child when they'd thought the child their own. This was beyond anything that she had previously known. She couldn't, she really couldn't leave

Jim, she loved him and their life together so much. Where would she go? Though her easy-going father would accept any situation her mother presented to him, Jean had made her feelings plain on what she called Sally's desertion of Peter. It would be impossible, should she become so desperate, to return to her parents' home. Was she being punished now for sins she thought she'd left behind? Surely not, for Elizabeth would be punished too by losing Jim as well. She thought she might destroy such hard-won happiness for them all... and now he could sit there like that, after all her nagging worries? She wouldn't let him get away with it and springing up and across to him, she cast the newspaper down on the floor to find him grinning, an ace from giveaway laughter, waiting for her to catch up with him.

Later that evening, as she put Elizabeth back in her cot, she saw the double crown of downy-soft baby hair as she turned her head to settle, and reached out a tender hand to stroke it.

She had meant to say softly "Goodnight", but what she actually whispered was "Goodbye."

Goodbye, Peter.